Dear Reader,

When my editor asked me if I'd do a twisted fairy tale for Harlequin Presents, I knew I had to do "Little Red Riding Hood." Not only is it one of my favorite fairy tales but I already had an image of a big bad billionaire called Jack Wolfe.

Jack was a cynical, scarred, ruthlessly driven alpha guy who could lure any woman into his bed but never wanted to keep them there... Enter Katherine Medford, my Little Red, who's as brave and, frankly, reckless as the fairy-tale chick (seriously, who visits Granny when there's a wolf loose in the woods?). But unlike Little Red, when Katie ends up in Jack's bed, she doesn't need some random lumberjack to rescue her, because she's all about rescuing herself...

One storm-tossed night in Granny's cottage, an accidental pregnancy *and* a marriage of convenience later and my fairy tale was getting a uniquely Harlequin Presents twist as Katie discovers it's incredibly hard to rescue yourself from a wolf, especially if you're starting to fall in love with him!

I loved adding a generous dose of passion, glamour and high-stakes drama to the old tale. I hope you enjoy reading it.

Love,

Heidi x

USA TODAY bestselling author **Heidi Rice** lives in London, England. She is married with two teenage sons—which gives her rather too much of an insight into the male psyche—and also works as a film journalist. She adores her job, which involves getting swept up in a world of high emotions; sensual excitement; funny, feisty women; sexy, tortured men; and glamorous locations where laundry doesn't exist. Once she turns off her computer, she often does chores—usually involving laundry!

Books by Heidi Rice

Harlequin Presents

A Forbidden Night with the Housekeeper
Innocent's Desert Wedding Contract
Banished Prince to Desert Boss

Hot Summer Nights with a Billionaire

One Wild Night with her Enemy

The Christmas Princess Swap

The Royal Pregnancy Test

Secrets of Billionaire Siblings

The Billionaire's Proposition in Paris
The CEO's Impossible Heir

Visit the Author Profile page
at Harlequin.com for more titles.

Heidi Rice

A BABY TO TAME
THE WOLFE

HARLEQUIN
PRESENTS

Recycling programs
for this product may
not exist in your area.

ISBN-13: 978-1-335-58354-3

A Baby to Tame the Wolfe

Harlequin Enterprises ULC
22 Adelaide St. West, 41st Floor
Toronto, Ontario M5H 4E3, Canada
www.Harlequin.com

Printed in U.S.A.

A BABY TO TAME
THE WOLFE

To my son Luca,

Who will never read this book, but whose childhood obsession with wolves and his gala performance in a Year 6 production of "Little Red Riding Hood" as the wolf led to my love of this particular fairy tale, and thus—eventually—my decision to write this story. I owe you one, my gorgeous boy—which unfortunately does not include a share of the royalties, just in case you were wondering!

PROLOGUE

Katie, I need your help! It's an emergency!

KATHERINE MEDFORD WRAPPED the large black trench coat around her red velvet cape to shield it from the spitting rain as she shot out of the Tube at Leicester Square while reading her sister Beatrice's eighth text in a row.

What was the problem this time? That Katie would have to fix? Because she was already late for her booking. And unlike Bea, who had their father Lord Henry Medford's considerable financial largesse to rely on, Katie could not afford to lose this job or the twenty-pounds-an-hour commission. The phone began to buzz. Katie's thumb hovered over the 'reject call' button as she dodged pedestrians along Charing Cross Road, en route to the children's bookshop where she was supposed to be reading fairy tales to an audience of four-to five-year-olds in ten minutes and counting.

But, as she went to press her thumb down, the image of Bea from years ago aged fourteen, tears streaking down her cheeks, her face a sodden mess of confusion and fear as Katie was marched out of Medford Hall by their father, tugged at Katie's chest. She sighed and clicked the 'accept call' button as she broke into a jog.

'Bea, what's the problem?' she said breathlessly, the corset of her costume holding her ribcage in a vice. 'I'm late. I don't have time for this, unless it really is an emergency—'

'It's Jack Wolfe,' her sister said, getting straight to the point for once and mentioning the billionaire corporate raider Katie had never met—because why would she, they hardly moved in the same circles. But she knew her sister had got engaged to him a week ago because of the pictures of Bea and her new fiancé all over the Internet.

An irritating ripple streaked down Katie's spine.

Wolfe had been hotness personified in a rough, untamed, wildly charismatic way wearing a perfectly tailored tuxedo. The mysterious scar on his cheek which marred his chiselled features and the tattoo on his neck—just visible above the pristine white dress-shirt—made him look even more darkly compelling next to Bea's bright, willowy blonde beauty. Katie would almost have been jealous of her sister, except she didn't have to meet Jack Wolfe to know he had to be a man like her father.

No, thanks. One overbearing bully is all I need in my life.

'He's invited me for dinner tonight at his penthouse on Hyde Park Corner, just the two of us,' her sister rushed on. 'And I'm scared he's going to want to take our relationship to the next level.'

Katie stopped dead in the street, her heeled boots skidding on the rain-slick pavement. Her fingers tightened on the phone as she registered the panic in Bea's voice.

'What do you mean, you're scared?' Katie gentled her tone to contain her own panic. 'Has Wolfe done something to frighten you, Bea?'

Wolfe was well known for being a rough diamond, with the looks of a fallen angel to go with his stratospheric rise from an East End council estate to the high-flying business circles in which her father moved. But Wolfe was also a big man, tall and strong, with a muscular physique that filled out his tux to perfection.

And that was without even factoring in the scar and the tats. How exactly had he got that scar which the tabloids had been speculating about for years? Was he violent, aggressive, dangerous?

Her own breathing became ragged as she was thrust back to a time long ago when she'd still been a little girl, hazy half-formed memories lurking on the edges of her consciousness. She swallowed down the wave of humiliation that those stupid nightmares still had the power to wake her up on occasion, struggling to escape something she couldn't see but knew was right there, ready to hurt her if she let it. She evened out her breathing… *Don't go there. Focus on Bea.*

'No, Katie, don't be silly. Jack's not like *that*,' Bea replied with more conviction than Katie felt. 'He'd never hurt me.'

'Then why are you scared of being alone with him?'

Bea huffed out a breath. 'Because he'll probably want to have sex and I'm not sure I'm ready. To be honest, I'm pretty sure I won't ever be ready. He's just a bit too much for me. He's ridiculously smart, and he can be very witty, and he's exciting to be with, but underneath all that there's an intensity about him. I have no idea what he's thinking. He's so guarded, it's like a super power. He's way too deep for me. You know how shallow I am.' Bea's manic babbling finally stopped.

There were so many things to unpick in what Bea had confided, Katie didn't even know where to start—not least because she absolutely did not want this much information about Jack Wolfe. But perhaps the most astonishing thing was the two of them hadn't had sex yet. While Bea was pretty flaky, she had dated before. And Jack Wolfe didn't strike her as the kind of guy to remain celibate for months while dating anyone…especially someone he'd asked to marry him. The guy oozed sex appeal. He could probably give a woman an orgasm from thirty paces.

So not the point, Katie.

'You're not shallow, Bea,' Katie said, because she hated it when her sister put herself down. That was their father talking.

'Whatever,' Bea said, sounding exasperated. 'But I still don't think we'd be a good match,' she added. 'At all.' She huffed. 'I'm worried I'll fall in love with him and he would never love me back.'

Say, what now?

'Then why on earth did you agree to marry him?' Katie asked, walking briskly again as she remembered the children who were sat in a book-store eagerly waiting for Little Red Riding Hood to put in an appearance. She was glad Bea wasn't in an abusive relationship. But she did not have time to debate her sister's confusing love life right now.

'Because Daddy insisted I say yes,' Bea murmured sheepishly. 'Jack has loaned Daddy some money on generous terms. If Daddy finds out I've broken it off, and if Jack changes the terms, he'll be furious...'

Katie's pace slowed again. She might have guessed their father had engineered this situation. Why couldn't Bea just stand up to him? But she knew why. Bea was scared of their father's temper tantrums, and with good reason... 'Surely you must know you can't marry Jack Wolfe if you don't love him, Bea?' Katie said softly.

'I know I have to break it off, but Katie, it's the pressure. Jack is very hot, but I'm sure he plans to seduce me tonight. And I'm not sure I'll be able to resist him. And once we've slept together it will be that much harder to dump him. I don't want to hurt his feelings.'

Whoa... What the...?

'Bea, you're not serious? Jack Wolfe has built a fortune on being an absolute bastard. His business strategy is to chew up smaller companies and spit them out. You said yourself you don't think he could ever love you. If the guy even has feelings, I'll be astonished.'

'Everyone has feelings, Katie,' Bea countered gently, making Katie wonder if her sister's airhead act *was* actually an act. 'Even Jack.'

'Do you think he has feelings for you, then?' Katie asked, the stupid ripple turning to a deep pulsing ache in her chest. What was that even about?

'No.' Bea sighed. 'He's very attentive. But he's not at all romantic. He pretty much told me he only asked me to marry him because he thinks I'll make a good trophy wife.'

Oh, for the love of...

'Bea, he sounds worse than Father,' Katie said, exasperated. At least Henry Medford had pretended to love their mother once. 'You shouldn't have let Father bully you into saying yes.'

'I know...' Katie could hear her sister's huff of distress even over the blast of a taxi horn. 'Which brings me to why I rang,' Bea added, her voice taking on a desperate tone that Katie recognised only too well, because it was usually the precursor to Bea asking her to do something outrageous or ridiculous or both. 'Could you go to Jack's place tonight at seven?'

'Why would I do that?' Katie asked. Did her sister need moral support to tell Wolfe the engagement was off?

'He's flying in from New York,' Bea said, bulldozing over Katie's question. 'But I told the doorman, Jeffrey, to expect you so you can wait for him in his penthouse—which is spectacular, by the way,' Bea added, her tone segueing neatly from desperate to wheedling. 'If you're there instead of me when he gets home, you can tell him I'm not going to marry him and I won't have to worry. Then I can tell Daddy *he* broke off the engagement.'

Katie stopped dead again. So shocked she didn't know what to say. Bea had asked her for huge favours before. Favours she'd almost always agreed to because she wanted Bea to be happy, and she knew her sister had a massive problem standing up for herself—thanks to their broken childhood.

Katie had always been there to stand up for

Bea when her sister's courage or determination had failed her. But this was...

'You have got to be joking!' Katie cried. 'I can't turn up at his place unannounced to dump him on your behalf. I've never even met the guy.' But even as she said it she felt the little frisson of something... Something electric and contradictory and wholly inappropriate rippling through her tired, over-corseted body. The same something that had rippled through her when she'd studied the photos of her sister and Jack Wolfe together a bit too forensically. 'Plus I won't have time to change out of my Little Red Riding Hood costume,' she added a little desperately. She lived in north North London and she was supposed to be reading fairy tales until six. Assuming, of course, she hadn't already been fired for being late. 'I won't do it, Bea. Absolutely no way...'

But even as she said the words the corset cinched tightly around her thundering heart and Katie could feel her fierce determination not to make an absolute tit of herself slipping out of her grasp.

Bea was her sister and if there was one thing she would always be prepared to do, it was her sister's dirty work. Because Bea had been there for her when she'd needed her most.

And there was also the matter of the ripple that was still playing havoc with her senses at the thought of a brooding, overbearing billionaire who was the very last guy on earth who should inspire a ripple in a smart, grounded, totally pragmatic, tycoon-despising woman like herself.

Perhaps she needed to meet the man to discover exactly how overbearing, arrogant and annoying he really was, and sort out this ripple once and for all.

CHAPTER ONE

JACK WOLFE GLANCED at his watch as the chauffeur-driven car pulled up outside the Wolfe Apartments on Grosvenor Place.

Five past three in the morning. Terrific. Only eight hours late.

He rubbed grit-filled eyes as he dragged his stiff body out of the car.

His contact lenses were practically bonded to his eyeballs, and he hadn't slept a wink on the plane. Normally he'd never take a commercial flight but, thanks to an engine problem with the Wolfe jet at JFK, he'd had to fit his six-foot-three-inch frame into a bed built for a skinny ten-year-old.

He checked his phone as he walked into the building and sent a half-hearted nod to the guy on the desk. He'd had no reply from Beatrice, but at least he'd managed to text her from JFK before he'd found another flight and postpone the dinner he'd had scheduled for last night. So she wouldn't be waiting in his apartment.

He stepped into the private lift that would whisk him to his penthouse on the top floor of the building and frowned at the floor indicator. Weird he wasn't more devastated about being forced to postpone tonight's dinner date. Perhaps it was time he addressed why it had taken him so long to fit seducing his fiancée into his schedule.

He liked Beatrice, a lot. And, as soon as he'd begun dating her, he'd marked her out as a perfect candidate for his wife. As tall and beautiful as a supermodel, she had a slightly kooky and admirably non-confrontational temperament which meant they had never had a disagreement. She didn't have a paying job, which meant there would be no conflicts of interest when it came to time management in their marriage—he was, after all, a workaholic.

And best of all, because of her father's position and her aristocratic lineage, she had the class and the social connections he needed to finally break down the last of the barriers still closed to him in the City of London and, more importantly, on Smyth-Brown's board—smoothing the way for the takeover he had been planning for years. So he could finally destroy the man who had destroyed his mother's life.

There was just one problem in his arrangement with Beatrice, though.

Sex. Or, rather, the lack of it.

She'd been hesitant to become intimate at

first, especially after she'd accepted his proposal. There was no rush and there was a fragility about her which reminded him rather unfortunately of his mother.

There wasn't much of a spark between them. But that hadn't bothered him either. He was an experienced guy with a highly charged libido. He'd lost his virginity as a teenager to a woman twice his age— and he'd had a ton of practice since at satisfying women.

The only problem was, after building towards the moment when he would finally make Beatrice his, he really hadn't been anticipating last night's dinner as much as he'd expected—in fact, it had almost begun to seem like a chore. He'd never dated any woman for longer than a few months, so he had been planning to suggest that they conduct discreet affairs once their sexual relationship petered out. But he really hadn't expected to feel quite so jaded before their sex life had even started.

His brow lowered further as the private lift glided to a stop on the fourteenth floor of the building. The bell pinged and the lift doors swished open. Thrusting his fingers through his hair, he stepped into the apartment's palatial lobby area and dumped his luggage next to the hall table.

He was being ridiculous. Seducing his fiancée wouldn't be a chore, it would be a pleasure, a pleasure which was long overdue. He was simply exhausted right now, and frustrated at the prospect of having to delay their first night together for another couple of days at least. He'd never had to be this patient before. Apparently there *was* such a thing as too much anticipation.

The ambient lighting gave the strikingly modern hall furniture a blue gleam, but he resisted the urge to request the main lighting be switched on. His eyeballs were so damn sore now, they felt like a couple of peeled grapes. No wonder he wasn't in the mood to jump Beatrice or anyone else.

Dragging off his tie and shoving it into his pocket, he headed into the open-plan living area. Floor-to-ceiling windows looked out onto Wellington Arch and the faltering stream of traffic making its way around Hyde Park Corner and up Piccadilly, the dawn creeping up to illuminate Green Park.

Calm settled over him, as it always did when he had a chance to survey how far he'd come from the frightened feral kid he'd once been. He adored this view because it was a million miles away from where he'd started in a squalid, one-bedroom council flat on the other side of London, ducking to avoid his stepfather's fists.

Rubbing his eyes, he walked deftly through the shadows towards his bedroom suite. He entered the bathroom from the hallway and finally managed to claw out his sticky lenses. He was all but blind without them and, after taking a shower in the dull light afforded by the bathroom mirror, he took the door into the bedroom.

Darkness was his friend, always had been, because he had once had to hide in the shadows.

Not any more.

The heady scent hit him as he closed the door to the steamy bathroom. Something spicy and seductive. Had Beatrice come into the bedroom before getting his message his flight had been delayed until tomorrow? When she'd never been in his bedroom before.

But it didn't smell like Beatrice. She had an expensive vanilla scent. This scent was far more arousing. Fresh and earthy—it smelled like ripe apples and wildflowers on a summer day. A wave of heat pounded south and made him smile. Even if he was so shattered he was having scent hallucinations, the instant erection proved he wasn't becoming a eunuch.

His groin continued to throb as he found the huge king-size bed in the darkness and dropped the towel from around his hips.

He climbed between the sheets, his exhaustion still playing tricks with his sense of smell. He closed his eyes, enjoying the deliciously erotic scent and the satisfying warmth in his crotch as his bones melted into the mattress. His mind plummeted into sleep and he found himself in a summer orchard, the ripe red apples heavy on the flowering fruit trees, the scent of earth and sun-shine intensifying.

Warmth enveloped him. The sound of a light breeze through the orchard matched his breathing, deep and even, and impossibly sensual. The ache in his crotch throbbed. A sigh—soft, sweet, hot—rustled through the trees and stroked his chest and shoulder as he lay in the sun.

He stretched, turning into the electrifying ca-ress, wanting, needing, more. His searching hands found silky hair, satin skin. He plunged his fin-gers into the vibrant mass and pressed his palm over velvet-covered curves, the tart apple fresh-ness surrounding him in a cloud of need.

His arousal hardened and the vague thought shimmered through his mind that this would have been the best wet dream he had ever had... But why was his dream woman clothed? And what was she clothed in, he wondered, as his fingers encountered rigid ribbing. At last he found the plump curve of a breast through soft cotton, the nipple pebbling as he plucked it.

The last of the fatigue melted away, his appetite intensifying, energy sparking through his body like an electrical current as he began exploring sweet-scented flesh with his lips, his tongue, his teeth. He nipped and nibbled, kissed and sucked, locating a soft cheek, a tender earlobe, a grace-ful neck and a stubborn chin... Gasping breaths feathered his face, urging him on.

His mouth finally landed on full lips to capture shuddering moans as voracious and needy as his. Fingertips, firm and seeking, caressed the taught muscles of his abs, sending the electrical sparks deep into his groin. His hands sunk further into the mass of curls and the delicious apple scent became even richer. He held his angel's head to take the kiss deeper, the summer sun warming his naked skin, shining off the plump red fruit and through the vivid green canopy overhead.

A wave of possessive hunger flowed through him as the stiff length of his arousal, so hard now he could probably pound nails with it, brushed more velvet. Was that a thigh? A belly? More damn clothing?

The earthy, erotic apple scent, the heady sobs and those caressing fingers ignited a firestorm that finally centred where he needed it the most.

'Yes.' He groaned. But then suddenly everything changed.

'Wait… Stop…' a groggy voice whispered close to his ear. Then snapped loudly, 'Get off me.'

The panicked cry sliced through the sensual fog like a missile, hurtling him out of the summer orchard and back into the dark apartment. He yanked himself back in the darkness, letting go of the mass of curls, hideously aware the warm, soft, body of his dream woman had gone rigid and become far too real.

'What the…?' He growled, the pain in his groin

nothing compared to the sickening, disorienting feeling clutching at his ribs. 'Are you really here?'

'Yes, of course I am!' came the hissed reply. Palms flattened against his chest, probably to push him off, but he was already rolling away, brutally awake now, his head throbbing, the painful erection refusing to subside despite his shattered equilibrium.

A barrage of questions blasted into his muddled brain all at once.

Had he just molested a woman in his sleep? And what the hell was she doing in his bed? In his bedroom? At three in the morning? Because this definitely was not Beatrice.

A dark figure scrambled out of the bed and a switch clicked.

'Argh!' He swore viciously, as the sudden glare turned his eyes to fireballs.

He threw his arm over his face, to stop his retinas from being lasered off, and yanked up the sheet to cover the still-throbbing erection. But not before he caught a blurry glimpse of wild russet hair and bold, abundant curves trussed up in a red and black outfit worthy of a lusty tavern wench in a gothic novel.

Was that a corset? Turning her cleavage into the eighth wonder of the world?

Horror and guilt gave way to shock and outrage as awareness continued to spit and pop over his skin like wildfire. Whatever she was wearing, it wasn't doing a damn thing to calm the inferno still raging in his crotch.

'Dim the lights,' he demanded of the house's smart tech system as his mind finally caught up with his cartwheeling emotions and his torched libido.

Was this some kind of a sick prank, or worse, an attempt at blackmail?

'Who are you?' he demanded as his temper gathered pace.

Whoever she was, it was not his fault he'd touched her. Kissed her. Caressed her... Good God, begged her to stroke him to orgasm... Shame washed over him and the erection finally began to soften.

He cut off the thought of what he'd almost done. He'd been virtually comatose. And he was the one who was naked. And he'd stopped the minute he'd woken up enough to figure out what was going on.

And this was *his* bed, in *his* place.

The lights dipped as requested, the only sound her laboured breathing and his thundering heart-beat as he slowly lowered his arm. He waited for his flaming eyeballs to adjust to the half-light. He couldn't see her properly, his myopia turning her into a series of fuzzy, indistinct shapes. But somehow, even without being able to make out too many details, he could sense her vibrant, vivid beauty—not classy and fragile like Beatrice's but raw and real and way too sensual. The earthy, spicy scent tinged with the ripe aroma of a summer orchard still permeated the room. Not a hallucination, then, but the smell of her.

Other memories flashed back to torment him. The feel of her lush curves—satin and silk against his fingertips—the taste of her still lingering on his tongue—heady and sweet and more addictive than a class A drug.

He thrust clumsy fingers through his hair.

'What the hell are you doing hiding in my bed?' he demanded when she didn't speak, letting every ounce of his outrage and frustration vibrate through the words. 'In the middle of the night...disguised as a Victorian hooker?'

'I'm not dressed as a hooker. This is a Little Red Riding Hood outfit!' The inane reply stumbled out of Katie's mouth, her whole body still vibrating from the shock of Jack Wolfe's touch. Firm, forceful, electrifying. Her mind still reeled from being catapulted out of heaven and into hell in one second flat.

Unfortunately, her body had not got the memo—that she was now in the most compromising, mortifying position she had ever found herself in in her entire life—and that was saying something for someone who had earned a living as a children's entertainer for the past five years.

Her nipples were hard enough to drill through

steel and the weight in her sex felt like a hot, heavy brick throbbing in time to her frantic heartbeat.

She'd been fast asleep, dreaming of him… Or so she'd thought. But now her panicked gaze devoured the man himself.

Jack Wolfe, in all his glory.

The snapped photos had not done him justice. Sitting up in his bed with a sheet thrown over the mammoth erection she'd had in her hand only moments before, Jack Wolfe was a smorgasbord of hotness laid out before her on thousand-thread-count sheets.

Her shocked gaze took in every inch of him in the softened lighting. The muscular chest, the broad shoulders, the swirling tattoo of a howling wolf which flared over one shoulder blade and across his left pec—only partially obscured by the sprinkle of chest hair that surrounded his nipples and arrowed down through washboard abs.

She jerked her gaze back up before it could land once again on the tent in his lap.

His eyes narrowed, or rather squinted, and she had the weirdest feeling he couldn't quite see her. His glare didn't alter as she took in the full masculine beauty of his face.

All sharp angles and sensual lines, his bone structure was perfectly symmetrical except for a bump on the bridge of his nose. And the livid scar which sliced through his eyebrow and marred his right cheek. His eyes were a startling, pure almost translucent blue with a dark rim around the edges. And horribly bloodshot.

She noted the other signs of fatigue: the bruised shadows under his eyes, the drawn lines around his mouth. Sympathy and guilt joined the tangle of emotions making her stomach pitch and roll. But at least it went some way to stem the flood of sensation.

'I don't give a damn who you're disguised as,' he finally snarled, the sharp tone cutting through the charged silence with the precision of a scalpel. 'I want to know what you're doing in my bed waiting to jump me in the middle of the night!'

'I… I fell asleep.'

'Well, duh…' The sneer broke through her shock and shame to tap into her own indignation—which had completely malfunctioned in the face of his extreme hotness.

However hot he was, she was not the one who had initiated Kiss-mageddon. Even sound asleep she'd known that was him. His firm touch skimming over her curves, cupping her breasts, tightening her nipples to…

She swallowed.

Focus, Katie, for goodness' sake.

'I didn't jump you…you jumped me,' she managed.

He scraped his fingers through his hair, pushing the short, damp waves into haphazard spikes. 'Fine, we're even there,' he said, the growled concession surprising her a little. Even naked—*especially* naked—he didn't look like the type of guy who backed down often. 'But I still don't know who the hell you are or what you're doing in my penthouse dressed as a porno version of Red Riding Hood!'

Porno...? What the...?

'This costume's not pornographic. It's not even revealing!' she all but yelped, her own outrage finally coming to the fore. *Of all the...* 'I wear this outfit to read fairy tales to four-year-olds and I've never had any complaints.'

His burning, bloodshot gaze skated over her and drowned her outrage in another flood of unwanted sensation. *Drat the man.* 'I expect their fathers enjoy the show even more than they do.'

She sputtered.

But then she glanced down at her costume. Okay, it had become a bit dishevelled during their dream clinch. She hooked the corset at the top, which she'd loosened before taking a quick nap in what she'd thought was a guest bedroom after getting Bea's text telling her she was off the hook and Jack wouldn't be coming home until tomorrow afternoon.

Wrong again, Bea.

There were no personal items in this room, not even any toiletries on the bathroom vanity... Who lived like that? she thought indignantly as she yanked up the cotton chemise under the corset so it more adequately covered her ample cleavage.

It seemed her quick nap had turned into a deep, drugging sleep before he had so rudely awakened her with his hot, firm touch and his voracious…

Seriously, Katie, focus, already.

She struggled to control the burn of humiliation. And arousal. Not a great combination at the best of times. She had to leave ASAP, now she'd finally gathered enough of her shattered wits to think coherently. But she still had a message to deliver.

'I'm here on behalf of your fiancée, Bea Medford,' she said, even though he was still glaring at her as if she'd ruined his night instead of the other way round.

'How do you know Beatrice?' he demanded, the frown on his forehead becoming catastrophic.

She opened her mouth to tell him, then snapped it shut again as her common sense caught up with her panic. The less this man knew about her identity, the better. He might have her sued or arrested. Even if he'd kissed her first, she was the one who had been in his bed, sound asleep at stupid o'clock in the morning. 'Bea wanted me to tell you,' she continued, ignoring his question. 'She's breaking off the engagement.'

The words dropped into silence and a dart of anguish pierced her ribcage. She hated to be the bearer of bad tidings, even to overbearing, staggeringly hot and arrogant billionaires.

But the pang dissipated when she noted his reaction. He looked mildly surprised, supremely irritated but not remotely devastated. And his glare—which was still directed squarely at her, as if *she'd* been the one who had just dumped him by proxy—hadn't dimmed in the slightest.

'I see,' he said. 'And she didn't come and tell me this herself *why* exactly?'

I know, right?

Katie quashed the disloyal thought. She was on her sister's side—*always.*

But it was impossible not to feel at least a little pissed off with Bea when she had to blurt out, 'She doesn't love you, and she didn't want to hurt your feelings.' She left out the bit about Bea's fear of succumbing to Jack Wolfe's all-powerful seduction techniques, because she had no desire to stroke his already over-inflated ego. Again.

Forget thirty paces. The man had almost given her an orgasm in less than thirty seconds while she'd been sound asleep.

Wolfe's glare intensified. 'Duly noted.' He growled without so much as a flicker of emotion.

So Bea had been right—Jack Wolfe certainly did not have feelings for her, at least not feelings that could be hurt. Katie's heartbeat took a giddy leap. She squashed it like a bug. Why should she be pleased by evidence that he was a heartless, manipulative bastard?

This man had proposed marriage to her sister without giving a hoot about her. When Bea was the sweetest, kindest, most beautiful woman on the planet…give or take the odd episode of unnecessary drama and the fact she was too much of a coward to do her own dirty work.

'Although that still does not explain why you were hiding out in my bed in the middle of the night, disguised as Little Red Riding Hooker,' Jack added, snapping Katie out of her revelry.

Little Red Riding…?

She stiffened at the insult, ready to fire something equally insulting back at him, but the scathing retort got caught in her throat when his glowering gaze raked over her outfit again. And what she saw in it triggered a new wave of heat.

'Tough,' she managed, her throat as raw as the rest of her. 'That's all the explanation you're going to get.'

So saying, she turned and grabbed the boots she'd left by the bed.

Time to stop bickering and run.

She heard his shouted demands—something about staying put and giving him a proper answer to his questions—as she sprinted out through the bedroom door.

She wasn't particularly athletic but, now her flight instinct had finally kicked in big time, she raced through the living area faster than a championship sprinter, grabbing her red velvet cape and raincoat en route. The lift doors were open, the lift waiting for her—*thank God*—and she made it inside and stabbed the button before she heard the crash of footfalls. The doors slid closed on the sight of two hundred and twenty pounds of enraged, spectacularly fit male sprinting towards her, wearing nothing more than a pair of hastily donned boxer shorts and an enraged expression.

She tugged on her boots as the lift dropped to the basement, then raced out of the building's garage. It was only once she jumped aboard a passing night bus heading towards North London that the adrenaline high caused by her narrow escape diluted enough for her to breath properly.

She was retiring as a children's entertainer as of tonight and finally moving out of London. She had enough money saved now, just about, to move the fledging bakery business she'd launched a year ago to the next level.

Her Welsh grandmother had left Katie a cottage in Snowdonia in her will—because she had always been proud of Katie for breaking free of her father's control. Angharad Evans had always despised Henry Medford after the way he had treated her daughter, Carys—Katie and Bea's mother. The mother Katie barely remembered.

The old cottage in the heart of the forest needed some work after being empty for years, but the beautiful forest glade where the smallholding was situated was like something out of a fairy tale, and satisfyingly remote. And the online business Katie had been building for over a year would be even better there, reducing her overheads once she'd invested in a new kitchen.

It was way past time she started making a life for herself that she loved. Instead of one where she was just squeaking by—and humiliating herself on a regular basis. And, if moving out of London and going into hiding in rural Wales also meant avoiding Jack Wolfe's prodigious temper, his hot body and any fallout from tonight, so be it.

CHAPTER TWO

One month later

'WHAT DO YOU MEAN, I can't drive to Cariad Cottage?' Jack Wolfe stared incredulously at the old farmer, who was staring back at him as if he'd lost his mind.

Maybe he had. Why hadn't he been able to forget the woman who had ruined all his best laid plans four long weeks ago now? So much so he'd finally hired a private detective to find her. And rearranged a ton of meetings first thing this morning to make a six-hour drive to the middle of nowhere just to confront her.

'Not in that, boyo,' the man said in a thick Welsh accent, glancing at the Mercedes Benz EQS convertible Jack had liberated from his garage at five o'clock that morning when he'd finally been given an address and discovered Little Red Riding Hooker was his ex-fiancée's older sister.

'You'd need a tractor, or a quad, maybe,' the farmer added. 'Or you could walk. Take about an hour—maybe two.' He glanced down at Jack's shoes. 'But there's a storm heading in.'

What storm? There had been no mention of a storm on his weather app. The sky above the treetops on the edge of the forest was startlingly blue, not a cloud in sight. Perhaps the guy was a friend of Katherine Medford—and was trying to head him off.

Well, you can forget that, mate. He had a score to settle with Miss Red.

He intended to get payback, not just for the broken engagement—which was now threatening to screw up the Smyth-Brown takeover—but for all the sleepless nights in the last month when he'd been woken from dreams of apple orchards and scantily clad wenches to find himself unbearably aroused.

Somehow, he'd become fixated on the woman. And he didn't like being fixated on anyone or anything. It suggested a loss of control he would not tolerate.

She owed him.

'Fine. I'll walk,' he said, tugging up the collar of his jacket and opening the muscle car's boot. He toed off his designer loafers and stamped on brand-new walking boots. He threw the car keys to the farmer, who caught them one-handed.

'There's two hundred in it if you keep an eye on the car for me until I return,' he said.

The man nodded, then asked, 'You want me

to send one of the lads with you for an additional price? So you don't get lost.'

'No, thanks,' Jack said. 'I won't get lost.'

He had envisaged this meeting in his mind's eye over four whole weeks and six long hours of driving. He didn't want company.

The farmer didn't look convinced. Jack ignored him and strode off along the rutted track into the shadow of the forest, the earthy scent of lichen and moss lightened by the fresh, heady perfume of wild spring blooms.

The storm hit forty-five minutes later, by which time his feet were already bloody from blisters, his face had been stung to pieces by midges and the phone signal had died, leaving him staggering about in the mud, trying to keep to the track.

The only thing still driving him on in his cold, wet, painful misery was the thought of finally locating Little Miss Riding Hooker again and wringing her neck.

Katie inhaled the lush, buttery aroma of chocolate and salted caramel as she lifted her latest batch of brownies from the oven.

She wiped floury hands on her apron. Only two more batches and she'd be ready to load the quad bike and drive her orders to the post office in Beddgelert. She frowned at the rain hammering against the cottage's slate roof and battering the kitchen windows. That was if the spring thunderstorm which had begun an hour ago ever stopped.

Heavy thuds broke through the sound of hammering rain.

Someone had come to visit? In the middle of a storm? How odd.

Dumping the apron, she headed towards the sound which was coming from the cottage's front door. Probably stranded hikers. It certainly wasn't locals, as they knew to come to the kitchen door.

Poor things, they must be lost and completely soaked. She'd treat them to a cup of hot cocoa and ply them with cookies until the rain stopped—she had to take advantage of every sales opportunity at the moment, given the woeful state of her finances. Who knew installing an industrial-grade kitchen in an off-grid cottage would be so expensive?

The thuds got more demanding as she rushed through the cottage's candlelit interior. The second-hand generator had died an hour ago. Thank goodness for her wood-powered Aga or her whole afternoon would have been a wash-out.

'Open the door.' The gruff, muffled demand sent a frisson of electricity through her. The memory flash—of a taut male body, translucent-blue, bloodshot eyes and a furious frown—was not wanted.

That was four weeks ago—in another life. Stop obsessing about your disastrous encounter with Jack Wolfe.

'Just coming!' she shouted as cheerfully as she could over the hammering.

Impatient, much?

But, when she flung open the heavy oak door with her best 'come buy my cookies' smile, the memory flash flared as if someone had chucked a gallon of petrol on it. And her smile dropped off a cliff.

'Mr Wolfe?' Her numb fingers fell from the door handle as shock reverberated through her system hot on the heels of the five-alarm fire.

Was the man of her wet dreams *actually* dripping a small lake onto her doorstep, his arms clasped around his waist, his broad shoulders hunched against the cold, his dark hair plastered to his head while he wore a designer business suit so drenched it clung to his muscular physique like a second skin?

Or was she having an out-of-body experience?

'*Mr?* Really?' he said, or rather growled, in that gruff tone that had a predictably incendiary effect on her abdomen. 'Let's not stand on ceremony, Red. After all, we've already shared a bed.'

What?

Horrified realisation dawned.

This is not a dream, Katie. Shut the stupid door.

But, before the shock and heat could recede

enough for her fingers to get the message, Wolfe had figured out her intention and thrust his foot forward.

The door slammed on his muddy boot. He swore profusely.

'Blast, sorry…' She cringed. She hadn't meant to injure him. *Much.*

He shoved the door open and marched—or rather, limped assertively—past her into her living room, trailing mud, rainwater and his injured dignity with him.

The muscle in his rain-slicked cheek, gilded by candlelight, twitched like a ticking bomb. But before she had a chance to ask what on earth he was doing in the middle of North Wales, hiking in a thunderstorm—in what looked like an extremely expensive and now totally ruined designer suit—he shivered so hard, his clenched teeth rattled.

And her shocked arousal got bowled over by a wave of sympathy.

While taking pity on him would have been a stretch because—even drenched and freezing, and with several nasty-looking midge bites he still had an aura of ruthless command which would have impressed Attila the Hun—she did not want the surly billionaire catching his death in her cottage or stomping any more mud onto her grandmother's handmade rug.

'There are towels and a shower through there,' she said, pointing towards the downstairs bathroom. 'Take off your suit and drop it outside so I can dry it by the stove. I'll find you something to wear,' she finished with more authority than she felt.

His scarred eyebrow arched and his sensual mouth curved into something halfway between a sarcastic grin and a suggestive sneer. 'You want me naked again so soon, Katherine? I'm flattered.'

He knows my name! Bea, you're a dead woman.

'Oh, shut up,' she managed, flustered now as well as panicked and confused and inappropriately turned on. 'Don't worry. I promise not to even *look* at your dignity this time. Let alone touch it.'

So why are you talking about it, you muppet?

Perhaps because she'd thought about it far too much in the past month.

Heat flared in his now laser-focussed gaze as it raked over her. 'Shame,' he murmured with a rich appreciation she did not have one clue what to do with.

She made a hasty retreat up the stairs to locate something dry for him to wear from the sack of her grandmother's old clothes that she'd recently washed to take to a charity shop in Bangor. Something that would cover his dignity and salvage what was left of her sanity.

Some chance.

She's stunning. Even more stunning than I imagined.

Jack allowed the thought of Katherine Medford's glorious curves in flour-dusted jeans and a worn T-shirt, her shocked emerald eyes, her pale, freckled skin and wild, red hair warm him as he peeled off his sodden clothing, dropped it outside the bathroom door and stepped into the snug shower cubicle.

The water pressure left a lot to be desired, but the heat was welcome as another shivering fit hit him. As he thawed out, his mind began to engage with something other than the visceral shock of Katherine Medford's unusual beauty.

Her cottage—its whitewashed stone and bright-blue gingerbread trim beckoning him out of the storm like a beacon—was cosier and more comfortable than he had expected from the detective's report on her finances. Thunder crashed outside as he dried himself off with one of the fluffy towels neatly folded on the vanity. The smell of apples from her shampoo reminded him forcefully of the erotic orchard he had visited nearly every night for a month in his dreams.

He dragged on his damp boxers, the only item of clothing which had survived the journey. And scowled down at the burgeoning tent in his shorts.

Behave.

She was everything he'd remembered and more—especially now he was wearing his lenses and could see her more clearly. But the resultant effect on his libido and his self-control was not good.

And worse was the way her saucy, sparky attitude affected him. Since when had he found defiance arousing? She'd slammed the door on his foot! And yet, as soon as he'd got inside the house, the thought of chastising her had taken second place to the thought of feasting on her full lips.

He sighed, rubbing his hair dry.

Time to get real. She might look harmless, but he already knew she wasn't. She would not get the better of him. *Again.*

'Here. It was all I could find that looked big enough.' He turned to see a toned arm appear at the door holding a…? He scowled and tilted his head. What was that? It looked like a piece of purple towelling with…were those pink ruffles?

'Great,' he murmured, lifting it from her outstretched fingers. 'Thanks,' he said, not sure he should be all that thankful. The arm immediately disappeared back behind the door.

'Would you like some hot cocoa?' the disembodied voice asked.

'I'd prefer coffee,' he said. Coffee was the least he was going to need to wear the monstrosity she'd handed him. He shrugged on the worn frilly towelling robe. It was tight across his shoulder blades and only just covered his backside. He looked ridiculous in it, but it was warm and dry and smelt of laundry detergent, with a hint of her. He'd worn

enough second-hand clothing as a kid to appreciate comfort over sartorial elegance any day.

'I'm sorry, I don't have coffee,' she said, sounding almost apologetic.

'Cocoa it is, then,' he said, then caught another
whiff of the delicious aroma which had enveloped
him when he'd first stepped into the cottage. 'And
a slice of whatever it is you're baking,' he added,
his stomach grumbling loudly as he realised he
was starving.

'The brownies are not for sale,' she said.
'They're already on order.'

'I'll give you fifty quid per brownie,' he said,
not joking.

He heard an astonished huff which made the
goose pimples on his arms—and a few other
things—stand to attention.

'Okay, sold,' she said, not sounding all that
grateful for his generosity. 'But don't think I won't
bill you,' she added with a sharp tone that made
him smile. He knew the value of something all
depended on what someone was prepared to pay
for it. And her mercenary zeal was something he
could appreciate.

'There's ointment in the cabinet for your midge
bites,' she added. 'It'll stop them itching.'

'How much will that cost me?' he asked wryly.

'It's free... For now, but don't tempt me.' The
door began to close before she added. 'I've lit a

fire in the living room, so you can sit in there once you're decent until the cocoa is ready.'

His smile sharpened as the door snapped shut, his usual confidence when it came to women, and especially this woman, finally returning full-force.

Decent? Is that really what you want? I don't think so, Red. Not from the way your eyes darkened as soon as you spotted me on your doorstep.

Maybe she had a more volatile effect on him than any woman he'd ever dated, but that didn't have to be a bad thing. When was the last time a woman had challenged him? Or made him ache, for that matter, for four solid weeks—enough to have him tracking her all the way to the wilds of North Wales and trashing his favourite suit?

Perhaps his obsession with her was much more straightforward than he had originally assumed. And just as easily remedied.

After tying the belt on the ridiculous robe, he found the ammonia-based ointment in the cabinet and began dabbing it on the bites on his face and neck, surprised when the angry swelling stopped itching.

The grin widened as he touched the robe's *froufrou* frills. No doubt Katherine had supplied him with this sartorial disaster to threaten his masculinity.

Yeah, good luck with that, Red!

It would take much more than donning a second-hand dressing gown to put a dent in Jack Wolfe's ego. And he intended to make sure Katherine Medford found that out the hard way…

He chuckled. *Pun fully intended.*

CHAPTER THREE

KATIE PERCHED ON the armchair opposite her un-invited guest and watched him devour his third brownie.

How could Jack Wolfe still look hot wearing her grandmother's dressing gown? Even the lurid pink trim hadn't dimmed his forceful masculinity one bit. Perhaps because too much of his magnificent chest was now visible in the deep V of the robe's flounced neckline.

'That's a hundred and fifty pounds you owe me,' she said, just in case he'd forgotten the agreed price. Instead of looking outraged, he smiled. Or was it a smile? It was hard to tell, the sensual curve as cynical as it was amused. She remembered what Bea had said about him being impossible to read. Her sister had not been wrong. The man was about as transparent as a brick.

'And worth every penny,' he murmured, licking the last of the caramel crumble off his fingertips.

Her heartbeat, which was now beating time with the torrential rain outside, sunk deeper into her abdomen. If he was trying to intimidate her with that sexy glint in his eyes, it was definitely working.

'So, what are you doing in Snowdonia, Mr Wolfe?' she asked, struggling to keep her voice firm—which required every acting skill she'd ever acquired. 'Assuming, of course, it's not an unlucky coincidence you turned up on my doorstep?'

She'd gone over all the possible motives for his appearance—from the bad to the absolutely catastrophic—while waiting for him to emerge from her bathroom and she couldn't think of a single one that might be benign.

Bea had rung her to thank her, the day after the night of the dream clinch, and said Jack had agreed to release her from the obligation without changing the terms of their father's loan.

Lord Medford had still been angry, but at least he hadn't freaked out completely. Knowing what their father was capable of when his plans were thwarted, Katie had been grateful, and also surprised Wolfe had been so amenable. But now she knew why. Obviously, he'd been planning to get payback on the messenger instead: *her.*

'No, it wasn't a coincidence,' he said, his intent gaze causing her goose bumps to get goose bumps. He placed his plate on the table beside the sofa. The pink trim on the robe caressed his pecs. 'I hired a detective to find you.'

She might have been relieved Bea hadn't ratted her out after all if she wasn't shocked at how determined he had been to locate her. Had she really injured his dignity that much? Because, as she recalled, it had been pretty robust.

His gaze skated over her, setting off more bonfires. 'I never would have guessed you and Beatrice were sisters.'

She bristled. She couldn't help it. She loved Bea to pieces, but she knew perfectly well that when men met her baby sister—tall, willowy, serene and dazzlingly beautiful Bea—they didn't notice Katie or spot the family resemblance. Unlike Bea, Katie was short, had insane hair and was, well, not exactly slender. She'd learned over the years to embrace her curves—and her chocolate addiction. She'd never be slim or elegant—she'd failed at a ton of yo-yo diets to prove it—but she was happy with who she was now and she was healthy and fit.

'Well, we *are* sisters,' she said. 'As much as I would love not to share any genetic code with my father, he insisted on a paternity test when we were both born to make sure we were his. Because that's the kind of trusting, charming guy he is.'

The muscle in Wolfe's cheek hardened. 'You don't get on with your father?'

'"Don't get on" is a bit of an understatement,' she said, proud her father's scorn no longer had the power to hurt her. 'We don't have a relationship. As a teenager, I wanted to be an actress. He had planned for me to marry one of his business associates. So he kicked me out of the house. It was tough for a while, and the actress thing didn't pan out because I didn't have the right "look",' she added, doing air quotes. 'But I've never missed being under his thumb.'

'How old were you when he kicked you out?'

She shrugged. 'Seventeen.' Perhaps he thought she was a fool to have walked away from all that privilege. From what she'd read about Wolfe in the business press, he'd never had any of the advantages she'd been born into. But she didn't care about his opinion. No one got to judge her life choices any more. That was the point.

'That's very young to be on your own,' he said, surprising her when the fierce look on his face became almost sympathetic.

Katie dismissed the giddy blip in her heart rate. She didn't need his pity. 'I wasn't totally alone,' she said. 'My *nain* was still alive then, so she helped me out.'

'Your *nine*? What is that?' he asked, pronouncing the word in English.

'It's Welsh for grandmother.' She glanced around the cottage. 'Cariad was her home. She left it to me five years ago, when she died,' she added, then wondered why she was giving him so much unsolicited information. 'And seventeen's not that young. I was older than you were when you ended up on the street.'

He stiffened, the frown returning.

Touché, Jack. Two can play the interrogation game.

'How did you find out I was once homeless?' he asked, his tone deceptively soft but with steel beneath. She remembered what Bea had said about how guarded he was with personal information. Apparently that hadn't changed.

'I did an Internet search on you after… After that night.'

The frown deepened. 'I didn't know that information was on the Internet.'

'It's not in the UK press, but I found an article written three years ago for a celebrity website in Mexico. They mentioned the rumours about your background while saying how much money you'd donated to a charity for street kids while you were there.' She'd wondered, when she'd read it, if the story had been planted to make him look good. Apparently not, from the way his jaw clenched.

'I see,' he said, then pulled his smart phone from the pocket of the robe and began tapping with lightning-fast thumbs.

She would hazard a guess that when his phone service returned *Estilo* magazine was going to be forced to take down the article.

'So it's true,' she murmured.

His gaze met hers as he pocketed the phone, the guarded look making the blip in her heart rate pulse.

'What is?' he asked evasively.

'That you were homeless as a child,' she continued, refusing to be deflected by the 'back off' vibes.

Shadows crossed his expression and the pulse of sympathy echoed in her chest. Moments ago it would have been impossible to imagine Jack Wolfe had ever been vulnerable and afraid and at the mercy of people more powerful than himself—and even harder to believe she could have anything in common with him. But, as she watched him debate whether to admit the truth or stonewall her, it became less hard.

'I wasn't a child,' he said at last.

'How old were you?' she probed, because the article hadn't been that specific. She'd simply assumed his 'early teens' had to be younger than seventeen.

Again she saw him debating whether to answer her, then he shrugged. 'Thirteen.'

'That makes you a child, Jack,' she said, stunned he could believe otherwise.

'Believe me, I'd seen enough and done enough—*more* than enough—at that age to qualify as a man.' He rubbed the scar on his cheek and the pulse in her chest bounced.

I wonder who gave him that scar?

'And I was certainly never a victim,' he added, dropping his hand. He reached across the space to snag her wrist. 'So you can take that pitying look off your face.'

His touch was electrifying, shocking her into silence when he stood and dragged her to her feet.

He was too close to her, his big body generating warmth, the scent of him enveloping her. Her apple shampoo mixed with a tantalising, musty aroma which threw her back to that night in his bed and into that unbearably erotic dream.

'I don't pity you,' she said, shuddering when he cupped her cheek with his other hand, pushing her wild hair back from her face and hooking it behind her ear. The gesture was disturbingly possessive, but oddly tender too.

'Good,' he remarked, his gaze roaming over her face with a purpose which made her more aware of his addictive scent and the heavy weight sinking into her sex.

'But I do feel sorry for that boy,' she said boldly, ignoring the renewed ache she thought she'd tamed weeks ago.

'Well, don't be. That little bastard is long gone.' His mouth lowered to hers, his eyes dark with arousal now. 'I'm a man now, a man who always gets what he wants.'

She should push him away, tell him to let her go, but she couldn't seem to move, couldn't seem to speak, all her senses focused on his lips and the memory of them skating over her skin, igniting fires which had been burning ever since.

'And what I want now is *you*, Red,' he murmured. It was an outrageous thing to say. They didn't know each other, they certainly didn't like each other, and it was fairly obvious he was still mad at her for what had happened with Bea…

But, even knowing all that, her heart continued to hammer harder than the rain outside as her body softened into a mass of molten sensation.

What was happening to her? She wasn't a virgin. But she'd never felt anything like this instant, insane chemistry. Her two boyfriends as a teenager had been nothing like Jack Wolfe. They had been friends, not a rich, powerful, ruthlessly driven man who was the complete opposite of sweet or generous or kind.

So why couldn't she tell him to get lost?

He framed her face with both hands. The rough calluses abraded her skin as he tilted her face up to his.

'You want me too.' His hot breath, flavoured with caramel, whispered over her lips. 'Say it.'

She flattened her palms against her *nain*'s robe, wanting to push him away. But then his ridged abs tensed beneath her fingertips.

'Tell me the truth, Katherine.'

'Yes,' she whispered on a soft sob of need.

Yes.

Triumph leapt in Jack's chest, her reluctant acceptance yanking at something deep inside. He slanted his mouth across hers, capturing her startled gasp, and threaded his fingers into her wild hair to hold her steady, releasing the tantalising scent of apples as his body ached.

The firestorm of need that had been propelling him here all along soared as her lips parted, instinctively giving him more access, and he thrust his tongue deep.

She tasted of cocoa and sin—silky, rich, delicious and even more addictive than her brownies. He explored in demanding, hungry strokes, while running his hands down her sides to capture her bottom and press her into his erection. He exploited each sigh, each shudder, scattering kisses across her stubborn jaw, biting into her earlobe, feasting on her neck.

Her kisses, tentative at first, became as fierce and furious as his. He draped her arms around his neck and drew her closer still, stoking the fire until it burned.

Feeling his control slipping, he yanked himself back and held her waist. Her eyelids fluttered open, her expression a picture of stunned arousal and shocking desire.

He let out a gruff chuckle, trying to ease the tension in his gut and calm the driving need to devour her.

'Where's your bedroom?' he asked, surprised he could actually string a coherent sentence together.

She frowned and he could see the wary confusion cross her face.

'What are you scared of, Red?' he coaxed.

Her gaze flared with outrage and a strange pressure pushed at his chest.

She really was glorious when she was mad.

'I'm not scared of *you*, that's for sure.' The fierce denial made her eyes flash with green fire. The desire in his abdomen flared.

Who would have guessed her independence was even hotter than those gorgeous curves or the fiery passion in her eyes?

'Then let's take what we both want,' he said.

It was a dare, pure and simple. A risky strategy for sure—and not something he would normally do. He didn't have to fight for what he wanted—not any more. Everything eventually fell into his lap, women most of all, because he always made sure he held all the cards.

But Katherine was different. Because he wanted her more than he had wanted any woman. She challenged him, excited him, pushed and provoked him. She already knew more about him than any woman he had ever slept with. The compassion in her eyes when she had revealed what she knew about his past had horrified him. And made him want to prove he wasn't that wild, angry kid.

No one looked at him with pity in their eyes. Not any more. He was the master of his own destiny now. And he intended to be the master of hers too.

The thought of how fixated on her he'd become should have made him extremely uneasy. But, as he watched her gaze flare with the same need and the same desperation, and felt her body soften, the fire in his gut became too intense to think about anything but getting her naked and ending this craving to finish what they'd started a month ago.

'Upstairs,' she said. 'First door on the right.'

He swore with relief, then grasped her hand in his and dragged her up the narrow staircase. He had to duck his head under an exposed beam to enter the low-ceilinged room. A flash of lightning illuminated a cosy, unashamedly feminine space. A brass-framed bed had been crammed into the small area and was covered with a home-made quilt and scattered with colourful cushions, the headboard draped with fairy lights. He flicked the light switch but nothing happened.

'The generator's out,' she said over the roar of thunder.

He marched to the window and drew the curtain, gilding the room in a watery light, but it was enough to see her more clearly, and that was all he cared about.

Untying the robe she'd given him, he dropped it on the floor, his skin burning from the sensory overload.

Her gaze darkened as it roamed over him, her breath shuddering out as it snagged on the tattoo he'd had done several lifetimes ago. He'd debated having it removed. The faded artwork had meant something to him once but seemed crude now, and vulgar on the man he had strived to become. But her avid gaze gave him pause.

How could he feel both exposed yet flattered by the desire darkening her eyes? He didn't need her acceptance or her approval.

Returning to her, he lifted the heavy fall of hair off her nape and cradled her head to tug her mouth back to his. Her hands flattened against his abs as he kissed and caressed the stubborn line of her jaw. 'You're wearing way too many clothes. Yet again,' he murmured.

Katie gave a throaty chuckle. 'I know,' she managed.

'Then let's remedy the situation.' Jack grasped the hem of her T-shirt and yanked it over her head.

It was his turn to feel light-headed as he took in the sight of her magnificent breasts cupped in red lace. Dark nipples poked at the sheer fabric, swollen and erect.

He rubbed his thumb across one rigid tip, gratified when she gasped and the nipple drew into a tight peak. He slid the bra straps off her shoulders, then unhooked the lacy contraption to release the abundant weight into his palms.

He lifted them to capture the engorged nipple with his lips. Tracing the puckered areola with his tongue, he choked down a rough chuckle when her fingernails dug into his shoulders. She clung to him as he worked one stiff peak then the other, kissing, nipping, tugging, her body bowing back like a high-tension wire. She panted, her uninhibited response even more exquisite than the feel of her flesh swelling and elongating against his tongue.

Keeping his mouth on her breasts, he released the buttons on her jeans with clumsy fingers and edged the denim off her hips enough to press the heel of his palm into the heat of her panties.

He groaned as his fingers slid under the gusset and found her clitoris, the slick nub already drenched with desire. He felt her contract around his invading fingers as his thumb caressed the bundle of nerves with ruthless efficiency. His own pain and need dimmed in the drive to make her shatter. Just for him.

She clamped down hard on his probing fingers, crying out as the wave hit with stunning force. He held her there, ruthlessly stroking until she slumped against him, limp and exhausted.

The scent of her arousal permeated the room, making his erection buck against his shorts.

I want to be inside her.

The fierce urgency joined the visceral ache. He stripped off the rest of her clothing in record time, then scooped her into his arms and laid her on the bed.

She stared at him, her gaze unfocussed, her breathing ragged, her red hair dark against the light quilt and her skin flushed with afterglow.

She was a banquet he wanted to feast upon for hours. But as he kicked off his boxers, and the painful erection sprang free, he knew the feasting would have to wait, because right now he had to feed the hunger clawing at what was left of his self-control like a ravening wolf.

He slid his arms under her knees to lift her legs high and wide and position the aching erection at her entrance.

'Hold on to me,' he grunted. Katie's hands clasped his shoulders as he thrust deep in one powerful surge.

Her sex massaged his length. So tight. And for one brutal moment he thought he would lose it. But, using every last ounce of his control, he held on enough to establish a rhythm that would drive them both towards oblivion. Together this time.

She opened for him, her body accepting all of his. His grunts matched her soft pants as she met his thrusts. The tide rose, barrelling towards him, and the pleasure and pain combined into a furious storm no less powerful or elemental than the one still raging outside.

Her body clamped down at last, triggering his own vicious orgasm. Shattering in its intensity, the climax gripped him as he soared into the abyss.

But, as he crashed to earth, two thoughts slammed into him at once as he collapsed on top of her.

I didn't use a condom.

I want her again already.

CHAPTER FOUR

KATIE'S FINGERS SLID OFF the broad shoulder pressing her into the mattress, Jack Wolfe's erection still solid inside her.

But, as the halo of afterglow faded, the shattering truth settled on her chest. And felt even heavier than Wolfe's muscular body.

What had she done?

She'd never made love before with such urgency, and passion and ferocity—he'd stoked it for sure, but she'd been a willing and eager participant in her own destruction.

He groaned as he rolled off her.

She flinched, aware of the tenderness from their brutal joining and the sticky residue he had left behind.

This man had been engaged to her sister only a month ago. And, even if he and Bea had never slept together, Katie had just crossed a line—an ethical, moral line. She didn't even like the man. And she certainly didn't trust him.

Perhaps she should be grateful they'd got the

hunger out of their system that had been building since that night. But her panic only increased when he shifted beside her and laid a possessive hand on her stomach. The heat didn't feel anywhere near as satisfying as it should have, but worse was that sense of connection which couldn't be real.

She shifted, attempting to scoot off the bed, but his hand curled around her hip, holding her in place.

'Where are you going?' he asked.

She was forced to look at him.

His tanned skin glowed in the turbulent light as the storm continued to batter the window. His strong features, marred by that jagged scar, looked saturnine, the unreadable expression doing nothing to contain the storm raging inside her.

'I need to wash up,' she said, horrified at the thought she hadn't asked him to use protection. She'd been blindsided by him, enough to lose not just her control but every one of her scruples and priorities. And that had never happened to her before. Not ever.

And they weren't even dating.

She grasped his wrist to lift his arm off her. He didn't protest as she sat up and scooped her discarded T-shirt off the floor. She tugged it on, feeling brutally exposed.

Bit late for that, Katie.

Thank goodness the T-shirt was long enough

to cover her bare bum because her panties had vanished.

As she stood, intending to lock herself in the bathroom until she could figure out how on earth to play this situation, he said softly behind her, 'I'm sorry. I should have used a condom and I didn't. I've never done that before.'

She glanced round, surprised by the apology and by the frown on his face that suggested he was telling the truth. The heat that shot through her already overused body at the sight of him naked and still partially aroused was not at all welcome.

He threw the quilt over his lap, but the lazy movement suggested he was doing it to protect her modesty, not his own.

Not that she had any. Not any more. Not after the way she'd thrown herself at him. And gone completely to pieces at the first touch of his lips, the first intimate caress.

'Are there likely to be consequences we need to address?' he asked, gathering his faculties a lot quicker than she could.

She shook her head. 'Not unless you have any unpleasant diseases,' she managed, so humiliated now she couldn't even look at him. She turned to stare out of the window, the sun finally putting in an appearance and making the raindrops on the forest leaves sparkle.

The cottage was in a small glade with a mountain stream at the back. One of the few memories she had of her mother was from here, smiling when Carys had brought her and Beatrice to Snowdonia to visit their *nain*. Before her mother had died and her father had forbidden them both to visit 'the old crone', as he liked to call Angharad Evans.

When Katie had arrived to clear the place out a month ago, she'd felt instantly as if she belonged here. But she felt lost now, disorientated, as if she'd become someone other than who she had strived to be—smart, independent and accountable to no one but herself. Had she also betrayed Angharad Evans' memory in the process by welcoming a man as ruthless as her father into her grandmother's old bed?

'I'm on the pill to help with my periods,' she murmured, grateful at least that by a stroke of luck an unplanned pregnancy wouldn't be a consequence. But then she wondered why she had explained the information. Jack Wolfe hardly needed to know she wasn't dating.

Perhaps that was why she'd succumbed so easily to the erotic charge which had flared without warning as soon as he'd declared an interest. It had been four years since she'd been intimate with anyone.

But, even as she tried to persuade herself her insane behaviour had been purely physical, she knew it wasn't. After all, it wasn't as if she hadn't had an orgasm in four years. She was perfectly capable of taking care of her own needs in that department. Although not even her vibrator had ever given her an orgasm—two orgasms—so intense she could still feel the dying embers threatening to reignite any minute just at the sight of Jack lounging on her bed like a well-satisfied tiger... Or rather, a well-satisfied wolf.

Wow, pathetic much?

'I'm clean,' he said, interrupting her pity party. 'I have a rigorous medical every year for my company's insurance,' he added, surprising her with his candour. 'And, as I said, I've never had sex before without a condom.'

'Good to know,' she said, trying to find the information reassuring.

'How about you?'

She swung round at the probing question. Outraged, despite the rational part of her brain telling her he had just as much right to ask her about her sexual history. 'I'm clean too,' she snapped. 'As luck would have it, I'm nowhere near as promiscuous as you are.'

He barked out a half-laugh, completely unperturbed by the bitchy response. 'Don't believe everything you read about me,' he said. 'I've become surprisingly discerning in my old age.'

The frank response made her wish she could take back the revealing reply as she recalled he had never slept with her sister. He'd been engaged to Bea for a week and had dated her for over a month. Why hadn't he seduced her sister with the same fierce focus he'd just seduced her with after meeting her exactly twice? And why should it matter when she'd stopped comparing herself to Bea years ago?

His scarred eyebrow arched and a speculative gleam lit his eyes, accentuating the dark rim around his irises. She had the hideous feeling he could see what she was thinking.

'Just out of interest, when *was* the last time you dated?' he asked, the forthright question slicing through her confused thoughts.

Heat scalded her cheeks.

Good grief, she'd never been a blusher, but she'd never met a man who was quite so direct. Or abrupt.

'A while,' she offered, not about to tell him the truth and encourage any more probing questions. Or, worse, declare herself the loser in the game of Who's the Most Jaded Person in the Room they seemed to be playing.

'Exactly how long is a while?' he countered, undeterred by her evasive answer.

'That's none of your business, Jack,' she replied, then realised her mistake instantly when a smile that had 'gotcha' written all over it appeared.

'So it's Jack now, is it?' He lifted his arms to link his fingers behind his head as he sat back against the cushions, revealing the tantalising tuffs of dark hair under his armpits and the roped muscles on the underside of his biceps that bulged distractingly. 'Progress, at last,' he finished, the smile now full of wolfish smugness, or smug wolfishness. *Take your pick.*

Was that his real surname, she wondered. Because it suited him almost too perfectly.

'We just made love,' she said. 'Even I can see the irony in still calling you Mr Wolfe after that,' she finished, struggling to gain some semblance of control over the conversation.

'Did we? Make love? Are you sure?' he mocked. 'How quaint.' The smile took on a cynical slant, which made him look even more jaded—and hot.

'It's a figure of speech,' she said wearily, suddenly tired of the banter and the knowledge she wasn't as tough and invulnerable as she had always assumed, or at least not where he was concerned—which only made this situation more dangerous. 'We had sex, then, if you prefer,' she added, trying to regain some of her usual fierceness in the face of extreme provocation. Did he know how shaky she felt right now? She certainly hoped not.

The smile became rueful, which didn't slow her pounding pulse in the least. 'Funny, because it didn't feel like just having sex,' he said. 'I've had a lot of sex in my life and that was… Well, different.'

Had it been? For him too? Despite his vast experience?

She squashed the foolish thought. He was toying with her, seeing if he could unnerve her even more. Why was she letting him?

She dragged her fingers through her hair and tied the wild mass in a ruthless knot as she glanced out of the window. The panic retreated as she noticed the storm had finally passed. The late afternoon sunlight struggled to peek through the trees. 'The storm's over,' she said, far too aware the storm in her gut hadn't abated in the least. 'Your suit should be dry enough to put back on,' she added, the hint so blatant even he couldn't miss it. 'I'll pack you some brownies for the road free of charge,' she finished, knowing she wasn't even going to hold him to the one hundred and fifty pounds he owed her. She needed him gone now, before she lost what was left of her sanity…and her self-respect.

She headed to the door, ready to hole up in the bathroom until he'd left her bed. And she could breathe again.

But as she reached for the doorknob his gruff voice sent unwelcome sensations sprinting down her spine. 'Not so fast, Red.'

She turned. He was still lounging on her bed but his gaze had become flat and direct, the muscle in his jaw twitching. 'I'm not finished with you yet.'

'Tough, because I'm finished with you,' Katie said with a conviction she was determined to fake until she'd got him out of the house.

She instantly regretted the bold challenge when the brittle light in his eyes sharpened and he let out a rueful chuckle. 'I wasn't talking about sex,' he said, the searing perusal making it very clear he didn't believe her for a second. 'Precisely.'

Her pulse began to punch her collarbone with the force and fury of a heavyweight champion. 'Then what were you talking about?'

'I have a proposition for you,' Jack said, the silky tone underlined with cold hard steel. 'One you won't want to refuse.'

She swallowed down the lump forming in her throat and locked her knees, the arrogance in his tone as disturbing as everything else about him. 'I don't take orders from you, Jack,' she said, determined to believe it. 'Even if we did just sleep together.'

It was a very long time since she'd allowed herself to be bullied by any man. And, whatever his proposition was, she had no intention of accepting it. He unsettled her in ways she had no control over, and that could not be good. But her curiosity got the better of her when she added, 'What's the proposition?'

He lifted his hands from behind his head and placed them on the taut skin of his belly, drawing her attention to the increasingly visible bulge under the quilt. Her gaze shot back to his face as the sensation sunk like a hot brick into her abdomen. But it was already too late, because his lips curved in that sexy smile that told her he had caught her looking.

'Go wash up,' he said. 'I'll meet you downstairs in twenty minutes. We should probably discuss it when we're both fully clothed,' he added. 'I would hate to take unfair advantage of you.'

She glared at him, knowing full well Jack Wolfe would have no qualms about using any advantage, unfair most of all. But she bit her lip, because calling him out on the blatant lie would be tantamount to admitting he *had* an unfair advantage. And being clothed before she challenged him again would be the smart thing to do... Especially after all the stupid things she'd done.

'Fine,' she said, reaching for the doorknob. 'But, just so you know, the answer is going to be no.' She marched out of the room with a flourish, slamming the door on his low chuckle, satisfied she'd managed to get the last word.

As she showered off the evidence of her stupidity, she promised herself that, no matter what his proposition was, however tempting, however tantalising, however hard to refuse, she would send him packing. Because she owed it to the seventeen-year-old kid who had spent a year sofa-surfing through London and doing crummy minimum-wage jobs on nightshifts to gain her independence. She wasn't about to lose it to a wolf.

CHAPTER FIVE

'WHAT DO YOU MEAN, *no*? You haven't heard the deal yet!' Jack stared at Katherine Medford, not sure whether to be frustrated or amused by the stubborn scowl on her expressive face. Although both reactions were preferable to the fierce tug of need she caused simply by breathing—which was starting to annoy him.

'I don't have to listen to the deal. Have you gone completely insane? I don't want to be any man's mistress but, even if I was going to do something as demeaning as that, it definitely would not be with you.'

Jack let out a gruff laugh, releasing the tension in his ribs. Katherine Medford really did look spectacular when she was mad, and she was practically frothing at the mouth now. He needed to get a grip on the effect she had on him. He'd never found argumentative women a turn-on before, but there was something about Katherine's spitfire qualities that fascinated him.

Go figure.

This fascination was purely sexual, though—for both of them—which surely made her even more perfect for the position he was proposing. A lot more perfect than her sister, anyway.

'Why not me?' he asked.

He had expected pushback and had been more than ready to counter it—after all, that was what negotiations were for. And he happened to be good at them. But her vehement rejection of his proposal was a little over the top, even for her.

'Because you're...' she spluttered, her cheeks suffused with that becoming blush which made the freckles across her nose glow. Something he'd noticed earlier when he had been lying in her bed, far too aware of her naked curves silhouetted against the window through her old T-shirt.

'Because you're *you*,' she said, as if that was supposed to mean something. 'Plus you were engaged to my sister about ten minutes ago. And I don't even like you.'

She leant against the kitchen counter where he'd found her after putting on his clothes. The trousers were trashed and the shirt hopelessly wrinkled, but at least both garments were dry.

His lips quirked. 'I'd say we just proved upstairs you like me well enough,' he said.

'I'm not talking about sex. I'm talking about everything else.'

'Such as?' Jack asked. This ought to be good. Was she a hopeless romantic? Under that guise of pragmatism and practicality? He had to admit he was a little disappointed. But he could work with that if he had too.

Perhaps it was pride, or perhaps it was the sexual obsession that hadn't faded despite their no-holds-barred antics upstairs—but whatever it was, he did not plan to take no for an answer.

She folded her arms, making those generous breasts plump up underneath her T-shirt.

'Such as shared goals, trust, enjoying each other's company,' she spat out, her brows puckering. 'Oh, and how about the biggie? Actually knowing more about you than I could find out in a few hours of searching online or ten minutes spent in bed with you? Such as that, maybe.'

So not a hopeless romantic, then. *Thank God.* Trying to persuade Bea they actually had a future together had always made him feel vaguely uneasy. At least with Katherine he could dispense with any semblance of hearts and flowers. He had decided that marriage wasn't necessary—Smyth-Brown's board could go hang on that one. He'd find another way to appease them long enough to get his hands on the stock he needed for a controlling interest. But having Katherine as his convenient date wouldn't hurt in that regard when he got her to London. She was still the daughter of a lord, albeit an estranged one.

'You spent *hours* searching for information about me online?' Jack asked, starting to enjoy her indignation when her glare intensified. 'I'm flattered,' he mocked, pressing a hand to his heart, even though the truth was he wasn't lying entirely. He'd have preferred her not to have unearthed information he had directed his legal team to have removed but, now she had, perhaps he could use it.

'Don't be,' she said. 'I was curious, that was all. I'm not any more.'

'Are you sure about that, Red?' He snagged her wrist, forcing her to unfold her arms. And felt her satisfying shudder.

She tried to tug free. He held on.

'You really don't want to hear me out?' he coaxed. 'Find out what I'm offering in return for your cooperation? You're in a much better bargaining position than you think.' Especially now he knew how much he enjoyed having her in his bed.

Getting this hunger out of his system, out of *both* their systems, wasn't going to be as easy as he had originally assumed. But, then again, their explosive chemistry would be a good way to enjoy their time together as he finalised the Smyth-Brown takeover and ripped the company Daniel Smyth's family had built over generations to shreds.

While he wouldn't normally have given his opponent a heads-up on how much he wanted to finalise a deal—after all, that was the biggest no-no when it came to deal-making—he could be generous with Katherine to have her where he wanted her.

'I don't care about the details. I don't want to live with you, I don't even want to date you, plus my life and my business are in Wales. It's completely absurd.'

'Is it?' He glanced at the gleaming kitchen equipment he knew she'd gone into considerable debt to finance. One of the biggest mistakes of fledging businesses was to be overexposed to debt in the first year. But her rookie mistake was his gain. He'd spent twenty minutes upstairs rereading the detective's report on the financial situation of Cariad Cakes Etc and he was more than ready now to go in for the kill.

'How about if I told you in return for your being at my beck and call for—let's say, six months...' that should be more than long enough to get this frustrating, insistent fascination out of his system. '... I would give you a hundred thousand pounds' worth of investment for your business over the next year for a ten percent share of the profits? And a ten-thousand-pound capital injection to cover your current debts.'

Her mouth dropped open, the bright, unguarded hope in her eyes making the slithers of gold in the emerald green glimmer. His chest tightened, surprising him. After all, he never got sentimental about business, and this would be—essentially—a business proposition. But even so he felt oddly deflated when the glimmer dimmed almost instantly.

'Exactly how co-operative are you expecting me to be?' Katie demanded, the brittle, defensive edge making Jack wonder about the young girl who had been forced to leave home to escape her father's influence.

He'd only met Henry Medford a handful of times, and he hadn't liked him—the man was an arrogant blowhard whose conservative investment strategy lacked vision and originality, and he had sensed that Bea was, if not scared of her father, then certainly determined to stay on the right side of him. While he didn't do sentiment, it was Bea's tentative attitude to her father which had persuaded him not to pull the Medford loan after their break-up.

He didn't sense fear from Katherine, but he could see her fierce determination to avoid the influence of any man would have to be overcome. Or at the very least managed.

'As I said, there will be some social requirements. I prefer to date women who elevate my social standing in ways money alone cannot.'

Not entirely true. He didn't give a damn about his social standing normally. But right now dating her would be useful in his quest not to scare off the Smyth-Brown board with what an inside source had told him was their concern about his 'lower-class background'.

'As the daughter of a hereditary peer—even an estranged daughter,' he added. 'You fit the bill.'

She blinked, looking momentarily stunned. 'I'm sorry…what? Did we just time-travel back to the nineteenth century?' Her gaze darkened with pity, making his temper spike. 'We're living in the twenty-first century, Jack. No one cares about titles and lineage any more. Especially not in the City of London. I think you're totally overestimating the importance of social status in your bid for world domination.'

'As you've never come from nothing, I would hazard a guess you know nothing about what it's like to be barred or blocked from your chosen path because of things you cannot change,' Jack said tightly.

'You're right,' Katie replied, the instant capitulation as galling as the sympathy shadowing her eyes. 'Maybe you can't change your past, or where you came from. But surely you're living proof it doesn't have to matter?' The hint of pity in the words loosened the leash on his temper still further. 'For goodness' sake, Jack, you don't even have a cockney accent. Why on earth would you need to date someone like me when you're a gazillionaire?'

He'd worked hard to get rid of his East End accent, he thought resentfully, well aware of the snobbery of his early investors who had been unwilling to put their money into the hands of someone who didn't pronounce their Ts and Hs properly. But he'd be damned if he'd give her more ammunition with which to condescend to him. He'd never been ashamed of his accent, or where he'd come from. He was just aware of how it had stood between him and his goals. And, anyway, having her seen as his date was nowhere near as important as getting her to London so she would be available when he wanted her.

'Frankly, we're getting off the point. I'm not interested in discussing the reasons why I want you on my arm at social events,' he said, resenting the fact she had managed to sidetrack him and touch a nerve he had considered long dead. 'All I'm willing to do is negotiate the terms of your acceptance.'

She huffed out a breath. 'Well, I'm not willing to negotiate it. I don't want to date you for any reason.'

The provocative comment was like a red rag to a bull, triggering every last one of his competitive instincts. Even if he hadn't desired her in his bed for the foreseeable future, her refusal to negotiate was enough to make him determined to change her mind.

'I think you're forgetting I lent your father a large sum of money on preferential terms,' he said. 'If I call that in, he won't be happy.'

Her eyebrows shot up, the surprise on her face almost comical. 'Really, Jack? Are you trying to blackmail me?' she asked, obviously expecting him to be ashamed of the implication.

He wasn't. In truth, he much preferred using the carrot to the stick when it came to persuading people to do what he wanted, but he hadn't been nicknamed the Big Bad Wolfe in the financial press for no reason. 'I wouldn't call it blackmail, simply a fact.'

Her eyebrows levelled off, her breathing becoming slightly laboured, which only made her more tempting. He clamped down on the inevitable surge of lust, while acknowledging that her inability to hide her response to him was another point in his favour.

'Call in the loan if you want,' she said. 'My father can't bully me any more. And neither can you.'

The bold statement demonstrated a bravery he admired, making it harder than expected to crush her rebellion. 'I'm not sure Beatrice would agree with you.'

She sucked in a breath as the implications of his threat finally dawned on her.

Distress flickered across her features, the obvious fear for her sister making him feel like a bastard, but he ignored the knee-jerk urge to reassure her. He'd given Beatrice his word he would not change the terms of the loan. And, while he could be unscrupulous when necessary, he never broke his word.

But Katherine did not need to know that. Using her concern for her sister against her was simply a negotiating tactic. He didn't need her to think he was a good man—in fact, it was better if she knew he was not.

Even so, he found it more difficult than he would have expected to remain unmoved when she hissed, 'You bastard.'

He shoved his hands into his pockets to resist the urge to touch her again. Crushing her spirit had never been his intention, but he always played to win, and this situation was no different.

You have to say no. This is insane.

Katie stared at Jack Wolfe, the strange feeling of unreality almost as disconcerting as the sensation rioting over her skin.

She loved Beatrice dearly, but it was time her sister stood up for herself. Katie couldn't protect her from their father's temper for ever.

And didn't she have the right to protect herself? Of course, the chance to clear Cariad Cakes' debts was tempting. But if she accepted she would be at Jack Wolfe's mercy.

Oddly, though, it wasn't the thought of the arguments and disagreements yet to come that bothered her. She'd already noticed a big difference between the way Jack Wolfe approached a negotiation and the way her father had bullied her. Jack might be commanding, powerful and ruthless enough to attempt to coerce her over the loan he'd made to her father but, weirdly, she also appreciated the fact he was being so pragmatic about what he wanted. Despite his outrageous suggestion, he hadn't condescended to her, hadn't tried to seduce her and had treated her like an equal. Something her father had never done.

She pursed her lips and crossed her arms over her chest to stop the pulse of connection getting any worse. And making her give in, when she knew it would be foolish even to contemplate becoming Jack Wolfe's trophy mistress.

Jack Wolfe was dangerous—not just to her independence but her sense of self. Because beneath the ruthless businessman was a man who could cut through her defences without even trying.

'Come on, Katherine,' Jack said, obviously tired of waiting. 'Is it really that hard to say yes?' he asked, the seductive tone reverberating in her abdomen as he stepped closer.

The hot spot between her thighs throbbed at the memory of him inside her—hard, forceful, overwhelming.

'It's only six months.' He cupped her cheek, the rough calluses turning the ripples to shudders. 'By which time, we'll have tired of each other. And by then your business and your future will be secure.'

She shifted away from the tantalising caress, her bottom pressing onto the countertop. She must not get carried away again on the tide of passion that had got her into this fix in the first place.

But, instead of crowding her even more, pressing his advantage, Jack remained where he was. He thrust his hands back into his pockets, almost as if he were having to force himself not to touch her.

And something flickered across his face. Something as shocking as it was unexpected.

Yearning.

But it was there one moment and gone the next.

She must have imagined it. Perhaps it was wishful thinking—making them seem like equals when they really weren't. She cleared her throat. Looked away from him. Night had fallen outside, but a full moon cast an eerie glow over the forest glen. Eerie and, compelling. And almost magical.

Snowdonia had given her strength, purpose and a sense of wellbeing ever since she'd arrived here determined to build a new life. But there was still something missing which had nothing to do with her financial instability or the endless stress of not being strong enough to make her dreams come true.

There was a Welsh word for the feeling of something lost, something longed for, connected to their homeland, that couldn't be directly translated into English: *hiraeth*. Her *nain* had explained it to her when Katie had been a homeless teenager but, being English, and never really having had a homeland she cared about, Katherine had never understood it.

But what if the *hiraeth* her mother had felt being away from her homeland, living with a man who had never really loved her, had been something like this deep tug of yearning? A part of her being she couldn't control?

Katie let out a slow breath, her heart galloping into her throat.

She turned back to find Jack still watching, still waiting, any trace of vulnerability in his expression gone.

She unfolded her arms, raised her gaze and ruthlessly controlled the hum of arousal.

'The answer's no, Jack,' she said.

Something leapt into his eyes that looked like regret. But she knew she must have imagined it when his jaw hardened and his gaze became flat and remote.

'Very well,' he said, surprising her with the instant capitulation. But then he stroked her chin with his thumb and the brutal sizzle rasped over sensitive skin.

She stood trapped in his penetrating gaze and regret sunk like a stone into her abdomen.

'But be advised, Katherine,' he said, his tone as harsh as the light in his eyes. 'I never give anyone a second chance.'

It was a warning that should have been easy to reject, but it wasn't, the foolish urge to call him back and say yes to his devil's bargain all but overwhelming when he took her quad keys, promising to have the vehicle returned that evening.

As the front door slammed behind him, her breath guttered out, her body collapsing against the kitchen counter. But the moment of relief did nothing to disguise the hollow weight still expanding in her stomach—which made no sense at all.

CHAPTER SIX

'I'M GLAD TO SAY the nausea is perfectly natural...' The doctor sent Katie an easy smile in the cubicle office of the small surgery in Gwynedd.

'How?' Katie asked, confused now, as well as exhausted. She'd been sick for the last ten days, every afternoon like clockwork, and it was starting to seriously impact her business. Because baking cookies and cupcakes and brownies when even the whiff of chocolate or vanilla essence made you puke was impossible.

It had been over two months since she'd turned down Jack Wolfe's insane proposition to become his mistress for six months. But nothing had gone right since the moment he'd slammed her cottage door behind him. It was almost as if he'd cursed her.

Sleep had alluded her for the first few weeks—florid, forceful, disturbing dreams tormented her every night in which he demanded her complete compliance and she obeyed without question. She could still smell him—ber-gamut and sex—on the sheets, despite washing them a hundred times. Could still feel his lips on her breasts, feel the hard, forceful thrust in her sex whenever she woke from fitful dreams. Then she had become tired and listless, falling asleep at a moment's notice, the thought of him always there, ready to jump her in her dreams.

The phantom sickness had almost been a welcome distraction at first to explain away the general malaise that seemed to have befallen her ever since he had left. This wasn't about Jack Wolfe and his insulting offer. This was about her working herself to the bone.

But in the last week, when it hadn't got any better, she had begun to panic. She couldn't afford to take any more time off work or she would lose her regular customers. She was on the verge of falling behind on her bank loans—and if that happened Cariad Cakes Etc would go under. But, far worse than that, if she lost the business she could end up losing her home, because she'd mortgaged the cottage to pay for the refit. The only upside was she'd saved money on her grocery bill because the last thing she wanted to do was eat.

The gynaecologist sent her a bright if slightly condescending smile. 'You're pregnant.'

'I'm...' The word dropped like a bomb into the silent surgery. For several moments she couldn't even process it. 'But that's not possible. I… I can't be pregnant, I'm on the pill,' she finally blurted out round the wodge of panic in her throat.

The doctor had made a mistake. That was all there was to it.

'I see,' the doctor replied, her brows furrowing. 'Ah yes, I have it here in your notes,' she added, reading off her computer monitor. 'Well, obviously it's extremely rare for this to happen. But no method of contraception is one hundred percent effective, even the contraceptive pill.'

'But…' Katie stared at the older woman, her skin heating under the probing gaze.

'Of course, if you haven't had sex in—'

'I did, but only once. And it was nine weeks ago,' Katie cut in, horrified by the blast of heat that hit her cheeks. 'But… I *can't* be pregnant,' she said again, her voice breaking on the words even as her hand strayed to her belly. Was this actually happening? Had she somehow got pregnant with Jack Wolfe's baby?

Tears prickled behind her eyes as the truth blindsided her.

If their moment of madness had left her pregnant—and somehow, where Jack Wolfe was concerned, it seemed more than possible—she would never be able to forget him for the rest of her life. And she hadn't exactly had much luck with that already.

The doctor's expression went from confident

to concerned in a heartbeat. 'Miss Medford, I did a blood test,' she said gently. 'You are definitely pregnant. What happens now, though, is of course your decision.'

Is it?

'At only nine weeks' gestation, you do have options,' the doctor added softly.

Do I?

Why did she feel as if she didn't have a choice, then? As if it was already too late? The sensible thing to do now would be to have a termination. This pregnancy had been an accident. A mistake. There was no way she could keep her business afloat if the morning sickness and the exhaustion kept up for another week, let alone any longer. And, even if she managed to get through the pregnancy without going bankrupt, how was she going to be able to run a demanding business while looking after a baby? She couldn't afford to pay for child care, or staff—not for a good few years yet, anyway.

But even as the fear and panic overwhelmed her she cradled her stomach and a surge of protectiveness swept through her. That morphed into something powerful and unstoppable.

She breathed out slowly to prevent her frantic heart beating right out of her chest. She'd never planned to be a mother—had never even thought of it. And now was the worst possible time for this to happen—especially with a man as ruthless and powerful as Jack Wolfe.

But what terrified her most of all was the thought of having her life ripped apart once again. The way it had been when she'd been seventeen—and her father had glared at her with hate in his eyes and told her to get out.

She blinked back tears and forced herself to suck in another careful breath… And think.

You've been at rock bottom before but you made a new life for yourself. A better life. By doing whatever you had to do to survive. Why can't you do the same again?

Another breath eased out through her constricted lungs but it felt less painful this time. She caressed her invisible bump.

Okay, kiddo, Mummy's got this. Whatever happens now, we're in this together.

It wasn't until she sat on the local bus back to Beddgelert twenty minutes later, her backpack stuffed full of pamphlets about everything from pregnancy vitamins to the benefits of breast feeding, that the full impact of what she'd have to do next knocked the air out of her lungs a second time.

I'm going to have to see Jack Wolfe again.

Informing the taciturn billionaire that she was pregnant with his child was going to be tough enough. Especially as she was fairly sure he would not be pleased at the prospect. He might not even believe the baby was his.

But what choice did she have? Not only did he have the right to know he was going to become a father, but she would have to ask him for help. She'd already maxed out all her credit cards and the next loan payment was due on Friday. She could ask Beatrice for money, but that would only be a temporary fix, and if her father found out Bea was spending any of her allowance on Katie he would probably cut her sister off too.

The idea of having to travel to London to-morrow, cap in hand, and beg Jack Wolfe for a loan went against every one of her principles. Given the insulting offer she'd turned down two months ago, it would also threaten to destroy every ounce of the independence and self-respect she'd worked so hard to gain since she'd been seventeen. What made it worse was know-ing she would be completely at his mercy.

After the endless battles with her father, being at any man's mercy went against the grain. And, having defied Jack once already, she wasn't even sure he'd have any mercy.

Be advised, Katherine... I never give anyone a second chance.

The rocky escarpment of Pen-y-pass disap-peared behind them as the bus travelled into the lush green valley of Nant Gwynant.

Jack might be forceful and overwhelming. But

what scared her most was how vulnerable she felt at the moment. If he knew she was pregnant, would he use it against her? What if he had found someone else to be his mistress? Would that be a good thing or bad thing? What if he demanded she get an abortion? He couldn't *make* her do anything, but somehow giving him the power to try scared her even more.

Of course, she wouldn't be able to hold off telling Jack about the pregnancy for very long. But why did she have to tell him everything straight away? Surely she'd be in a better bargaining position if he didn't know? Asking him to reconsider the offer of financial help for her business would be hard. Especially as she wasn't even sure any more whether or not she wanted to be his mistress.

After all, however adamant she'd been two months ago, she still hadn't forgotten the effect he had on her—not even close. But telling him about the pregnancy and throwing herself on his mercy—or lack of it—felt so much more risky.

This was just another negotiation, she told herself staunchly, but it was one she had to make work for her and her baby and her business. The last thing she should do, given what a skilful negotiator Jack was, was give him an even stronger bargaining position.

'Mr Wolfe, there's a Miss Medford downstairs in reception. She doesn't have an appointment, but she insists she knows you, and the front desk asked me to check with you first before they send her away.'

Jack's head lifted at his PA Gorinda's comment. The bump of exhilaration annoyed him. 'Do you know *which* Miss Medford?'

'No, Mr Wolfe, but apparently she's been very persistent.'

'Uh-huh,' he murmured as the bump went nuts.

It had to be Katherine. He hadn't spoken to Beatrice since she'd broken off their engagement, and she didn't have the guts to come to his office without an appointment. Katherine, on the other hand...

'I did tell them there was no way you would—'

'It's okay, Gorinda.' He cut her off. 'Have them send her up.'

Gorinda disguised her astonishment with a quick nod, like the first-class professional she was.

As Jack waited for Katherine to arrive, he got up and paced across the office. He should have told her to go to hell. She'd rejected his offer two months ago now. He'd intended to forget her as soon as he strolled out of her cottage. To find someone else. But it hadn't quite worked out that way. Not only had he not been able to forget her, no other woman had come close to exciting him the way she did.

None of them had Katherine's vibrant hair, her lush curves, her quick wit or her sharp, intelligent emerald eyes. And not one of them made him ache.

He'd come to the conclusion that, if he couldn't have her, he didn't want anyone else. Which was infuriating.

How had she captivated him so comprehensively? When her rejection still stung, reminding him of the feral kid he'd once been…? On the outside, not wanted and never to be invited in.

He returned to his desk, determined not to let her see his agitation—or his excitement at the thought of seeing her again.

Several eternities later, Gorinda stepped into the office with Katherine. After announcing his uninvited guest, his PA left and shut the door.

He took his time staring at the woman who still occupied far too much of his head space.

In a tailored pencil skirt, a silk blouse and low heels, her wild hair pinned on top of her head in a ruthless up-do, she looked more sophisticated than he'd ever seen her. But the power suit and heels couldn't disguise her lush curves or dewy skin. Or the way the buttons of her blouse strained against her cleavage. Was he imagining it, or did her breasts look even more spectacular than he remembered?

'Hello, Katherine,' he said, his tone huskier than he would have liked. He remained seated, keeping his expression flat and direct, even as the bump in his heart rate accelerated. 'To what do I owe the unexpected pleasure?' he added, doing nothing to hide the slice of sarcasm in his tone.

Her cheeks turned a delectable shade of pink. The inconvenient arousal flowed south.

Damn, I still want her—too much.

He shifted in his seat, the sudden recollection of wrapping his lips around those hard, swollen peaks aggravating his temper, not to mention the ache in his pants.

The sour taste in his mouth wasn't far behind, though. She had to be here to renegotiate his offer. Why he should be surprised, he had no idea. But what surprised him more was his disappointment. She'd rejected him when he'd offered her a generous deal two months ago. He'd told her then she wouldn't get a second chance and he still meant it. However much he might still want her.

'Hello, Jack,' she said. 'Can I sit down?'

He swept his hand towards the leather armchair on the other side of the desk. 'Go ahead. You've got five minutes to say whatever you came to say,' he said, gratified by the flash of annoyance before she managed to mask it.

Damned if he didn't still find her rebelliousness a major turn-on.

But as she crossed the room and sat down

he frowned. Had she lost weight? Because he could still recall every luscious inch of her in far too much detail and, apart from her breasts, her curves didn't look as much of a handful as he remembered. Not only that, but she moved stiffly, without the confident energy of two months ago.

As her face caught the sun streaming through the office windows, he noticed the tight line of her lips and the bruised shadows under her eyes that she'd tried to mask with make-up.

He stifled the concern pushing against his chest and forced it into a box marked 'not your problem'.

She'd probably been working herself to the bone to make a go of her failing business. But why should he care? He'd offered her a way out. And she'd thrown it back in his face.

He glanced at his watch. 'You've got four minutes now,' he said.

'I wanted to ask about the financing you mentioned two months ago.' She leaned forward, offering him an even better view of her cleavage—which had to be deliberate. 'It's been...' She sighed, the gushing breath weary. 'More of a challenge than I thought to keep up payments on my loans. If you're still interested in investing, I could offer you twenty-five percent instead of ten.'

His disappointment at the evidence that she could be bought after all was tempered by the surge of triumph. He had her where he wanted her now. But he'd be damned if he'd give her an easy ride. 'And the deal I discussed?'

'I'd be willing to do that too, of course,' she said without a moment's hesitation. 'With the six-month time limit you mentioned, obviously.'

'And what exactly would you be prepared to do for this investment?' he asked, keeping his gaze fixed firmly on the blush which was now spreading across her neck.

'Whatever you want me to do,' she said softly.

His chest tightened with anger. 'Uh-huh,' he ground out, holding on to his fury with an effort. 'And what do you envisage that entailing?'

He'd intended to pay to relocate her to London for six months, because their affair would have to be at his convenience, not hers. But if they had decided to sleep together—to get this damn chemistry out of their system—he had never intended to buy her cooperation in that regard. But she'd never given him the chance to explain any of that two months ago. She'd simply jumped to the conclusion he would be paying her for sex—and had rejected him out of hand.

He steepled his fingers to stop them shaking as the fury started to consume him. 'And if I said I didn't just want to date you socially? That I wanted you in my bed for the duration? What then?' he asked, finally pushing the point.

Her eyes widened, the flash of anxiety going some way to satisfy his sense of outrage.

That's right, Red, let's see how far you're willing to go!

Her face fell, the blush blazing now as the last of the eager hope he had glimpsed died. He'd shocked her. And insulted her. Just as he'd intended.

But just as he was sure she would finally realise how insulting that proposition was, to both of them, she said, 'Okay, if that's what you want.'

The anger flared, but right behind it was astonishment. And that heady shot of arousal still throbbing in his groin.

How could he still want her when she was only offering herself in exchange for payment? Had her outrage at the cottage all been an act?

Of course it had, he thought viciously, surprised to realise he actually felt disillusioned when he'd figured he had lost all his illusions years ago.

He was a deeply cynical guy because he'd had to be. He'd come from the very bottom and made it to the top. And he'd had to fight like hell to scale every rung of that ladder. He couldn't afford sentimentality or loyalty unless it benefitted his bottom line.

But although he'd been angry when he'd walked away from her—because she'd denied him something he wanted—in the weeks since he'd been captivated by the notion that Katherine Medford might actually be the real deal. Someone prepared to put their dignity and self-respect before money. And status. And benefitting their own bottom line.

The sour taste in his mouth made his lips twist in a cruel smile. 'I see,' he said, letting his gaze roam over her, the perusal deliberately insulting as he got up from his desk. He walked towards her, suddenly determined to punish her for destroying the image he'd had of her... And get some much-needed payback for the snub that had bruised his ego more than it should have.

What a fool he'd been, wasting months getting hung up on a woman who didn't even exist.

He beckoned her out of the seat. She stood, wary eyes searching his face, her magnificent breasts rising up and down with her staggered breathing.

She chewed on her lip while her deep-green eyes dilated to black. Satisfaction flowed through him.

'What...what do you want?' She wrapped her arms around her waist, holding in her shudder of response, but he could see the peaks of her breasts standing to attention beneath her blouse.

Red, we both know you want me as much as I want you.

He let the cruel smile spread, damned if he

was going to leave her with any pride. People had thought they were better than him his whole life. And he'd taken great pleasure in proving them wrong. She was no different from all the rest.

He leaned closer, close enough to take in a lungful of her tantalising scent—apples and earth and pure, unadulterated sin. The burgeoning erection hardened enough to brush against her belly and he heard her sharp intake of breath, felt the judder of reaction course through her body.

He shoved his fists into his pockets, determined not to touch, not to take. This time she was going to come to him.

'I want you to show me what you've got,' he whispered against her neck. 'That's worth a hundred grand of my money, Red.'

He straightened away from her.

Her expressive features tightened and resentment sparkled in her eyes, highlighting the shards of gold in the emerald green.

There she is.

His breath clogged his lungs and desire flared, crackling in the air between them like an electric force field. But, before he had a chance to register the jolt of excitement, she lifted her arms and grasped his shoulders.

Her fingernails trailed across his nape, sending arrows of sensation shooting through his spine, straight down to his groin. And then she lifted her face to his, offering herself with a boldness, a determination, that robbed him of breath before she rose up on tiptoes and pressed her lips to his in a defiant kiss.

Elemental need exploded like a firework display in his gut, and all thoughts of payback, of punishment, were obliterated by the furious juggernaut of desire too long denied.

Her lips opened on a staggered breath and he thrust his tongue deep, capturing each startled sob of her surrender. He yanked his clenched fists out of his pockets and grasped her hips to pull her vibrating body against the brutal ridge in his trousers. He ground the erection against her, each stroke of his tongue, each brush of his shaft, driving him closer to the edge.

His hands skimmed up her side and cradled her breasts. She bowed back and he dragged his mouth down to suckle the frantic beat in her neck. He fumbled with her blouse, giving a staggered groan as the buttons popped. Lifting the fragrant flesh free of its lacy prison, he traced the engorged peak with his lips but, as he trapped the swollen flesh against the roof of his mouth and suckled hard, she bucked in his arms and cried out—the shocked gasp one of pain, not pleasure.

What the...?

'Ow!'

Her distress doused the fire and he released

her so abruptly, she staggered backwards. He caught her elbow before she could fall over the armchair.

'How...?' he managed, his pulse thundering so hard in his ears he was struggling to hear, let alone think.

What had just happened? One minute they had been devouring each other, and then...

She tugged her arm free, her movements jerky, frantic, her eyes downcast, her body shaking with the same tremors wracking his own. He watched her gather the remnants of her blouse. The blouse he'd torn off her.

'Did I hurt you?' he asked, his voice raw.

How the hell had everything got out of control so quickly? He'd been ready to take her right here in his office. The point he'd been trying to make—which seemed petulant and pointless now—was instantly forgotten in the maelstrom of needs triggered by her glorious defiance and the touch of her lips on his.

She shook her head, but her chin remained tucked into her chest and he couldn't see her face. She was still shaking, her knuckles whitening on the torn silk.

Guilt washed through him. He tucked his thumb under her chin and drew her face up to his. 'Katherine, did I hurt you?' he asked again.

Her eyes—that deep, vibrant emerald—were mossy with distress, but devoid of the accusation he had been expecting. 'No,' she murmured, the apologetic tone only confusing him more. 'It's just, I'm a lot more sensitive there.'

His gaze dipped to her full breasts now plumped up under her tightly folded arms. 'Okay,' he said, still trying to figure out where that cry of pain had come from.

'Oh, God,' she whispered, clasping her hand over her mouth. 'Where's the nearest toilet?'

Her features drew tight, a sheen of sweat popping out on her brow, her face turning grey beneath the impressive beard burn starting to appear on her cheeks.

'What?' he asked, the concern he'd tried to contain earlier expanding like a beach ball in his gut.

'Your nearest toilet, Jack!' Her voice rose in distress. 'Where is it?' she cried. 'I'm going to throw up!'

He pointed to the office's large *en suite* bathroom, shocked and confused now, as well as extremely turned on.

She shot out of the room so fast, an apple-scented breeze feathered across his face. Two seconds later, the sounds of violent retching echoed around the silent office.

What the hell is going on?

He walked across the carpeted floor, propped his shoulder against the door jamb, the beach ball expanding as he watched her bent over the toilet bowl, puking her guts up.

He supposed he ought to be offended, embarrassed even, that his lovemaking had made her violently ill. But he was still reeling from the sudden shift from incendiary lust to total disaster—and the feeling he'd just been kicked into another dimension without warning.

The erection finally deflated—mercifully.

Perhaps he shouldn't be surprised, given Katherine had a habit of bringing enough drama into his life to put a TV soap opera to shame. But, as he rinsed a face cloth out in the sink, confusion gave way to curiosity and concern. And a ton of unanswered questions bombarded him all at once.

Why had she come here? And, more importantly, why *now*? Because her motives didn't seem nearly as straightforward as he'd assumed. If she was really an opportunist, an unscrupulous femme fatale prepared to sell her body to rescue her business, why hadn't she agreed to become his mistress two months ago?

The gruesome retching finally subsided and she collapsed onto her bottom. Sitting cross-legged on the floor, she didn't just look tired, she looked shattered and fragile. In a way she never had before. Fragile, defensive and…guilty.

What did she have to feel guilty about?

He handed her the cool cloth, ignoring the residual buzz as their fingers brushed.

'Thank you,' she said, wiping her mouth before folding the cloth with infinite care and pressing it to her burning cheeks. 'It's okay, that's the worst of it over,' she murmured, as if this had happened before.

He crouched beside her, unable to resist the urge to swipe his finger across her clammy forehead and tuck a stray strand of hair behind her ear. She trembled, but didn't draw away from his touch. Her gaze met his at last. The guilty flush highlighted her pale cheeks.

His what-the-hell-ometer shot into the red zone and the wodge of confusion and concern threatened to gag him.

'Why did you come to me?' he demanded, his guts tying into tight, greasy knots. Was she seriously ill?

'I told you, I need money to save my business,' she said, but she ducked her head again.

'Don't give me that crap,' he said, annoyed with her now, as well as himself. Why had he believed so readily that the bold, beautiful, belligerent and stunningly defiant woman he had left behind in Wales had become some conniving little gold-digger in the space of a few months?

He grasped her chin, losing his patience as the sense of detachment, cynicism and ruthlessness which he had relied on for so long became dull and discordant. He shouldn't care why she was here, why she needed his money so badly, but he did.

'Tell me the truth. Are you seriously ill?' he asked.

She puffed out a breath. 'No.'

The relief he wanted to feel didn't come. 'Then why did you just lose your lunch in my toilet?'

The guilty flush became so vivid it would probably be visible from Mars. 'Because I'm pregnant,' she replied. 'With your child.'

CHAPTER SEVEN

'YOU... WHAT?' JACK murmured, his voice rough with shock, and Katie watched his gaze drop to her belly.

Katie's still tender stomach flipped over as his knees dropped to the bathroom tiles, his balance shot, as well as his usual cast-iron control.

'It was an accident,' she said. 'I can take a DNA test once it's born, if you don't believe it's yours,' she added, expecting to see suspicion, even accusation, on his face.

When his gaze rose, though, he still looked dazed. But then two creases appeared between his brows.

She braced, ready for anger, but all he said was, 'How long have you known?'

'Since yesterday,' she replied. 'I'd been sick on and off for two weeks and it was affecting my work.' She knew she was babbling, but she couldn't seem to stop, wanting to fend off the accusations that were bound to come soon. He'd treated her with contempt as soon as she'd arrived. Which only made her more determined to hold her ground, to get what she needed before he found out how much she needed it.

But his expression remained oddly unreadable.

'It's not easy baking when even the scent of food makes you nauseous,' she finished.

'No doubt,' he said, his gaze drifting back to her belly. 'I thought you were on the pill.'

Oddly, the question lacked the cynicism she'd expected, but even so she went on the offensive.

'I *was* on the pill. But it was low-dosage and I'd only been on it for a week. Even so, the doctor said it's extremely rare.' Feeling stronger, she added an edge to her voice. 'It seems you have extremely fertile sperm.'

'Who knew?' His lips quirked, the hint of wry amusement surprising her even more. Did he think this was funny? But as he continued to study her in that unnerving way he had, as if he could see past every one of her defences, his brow furrowed again. 'Why didn't you tell me about the pregnancy as soon as you arrived?'

She cursed her pale skin as the tell-tale heat crawled up her neck.

'Because I didn't want to get the third degree about how it had happened. Or have you try to talk me into an abortion,' she said, knowing she had been right not to blurt out the truth and give him even more power to hurt her.

Anger spread up her chest to disguise the hurt as she recalled the insulting way he'd treated her. Had he even really still wanted her? Or had he simply intended to humiliate her, get her to show him how much she still wanted him, before he slapped her down?

She'd put everything into that kiss, had lost herself in it seconds after he'd responded, but had he? She wasn't even sure about that any more. Had it all been a game to him to make her go insane with lust just so he could humiliate her more when he rejected her?

'What the hell makes you think I'd try to force you to have an abortion?' he asked, surprising her again. Because he didn't look superior or in control any more. He looked furious.

'Because...' She sputtered to a stop. He actually looked really offended. 'Well, aren't you?' she managed, her righteousness faltering a little.

'Do you want to have the child?' he asked.

Emotion closed her throat. The baby felt so real to her now, even though, according to all the research she'd done in the last twenty-four hours, it was no bigger than a grain of rice.

'Yes, I do want it, very much,' she said without hesitation around the thickness in her throat.

'Then I will support your choice,' Jack answered without an ounce of sarcasm. Or even any apparent resentment.

Katie's jaw went slack. To say she was sur-

prised by the statement would be a massive understatement. She wasn't just surprised—she
was stunned speechless.

'Really?' she whispered at last. 'You're not
angry?' she asked, not sure she could believe
him as she struggled to contain the painful hope
pressing against her chest wall.

Was this just another trick? Surely it had to
be? She would have expected a man as cynical
as him to feel trapped, or at the very least suspicious. She certainly had not expected him to
so readily believe not only that the baby was
his, but that her pregnancy had genuinely been
an accident.

'I pay for my mistakes,' Jack said. 'And this
is my fault, not yours. I should have worn protection and I didn't.'

Our baby is not a mistake.

It was what she wanted to say. But as she
opened her mouth to protest Jack stood up and,
taking her elbow, pulled her to her feet.

'I do have some conditions, though.'

'What conditions?' She stared at him, trying to decipher what was coming so she could
ward it off... But as usual his expression gave
nothing away.

How could he be so controlled when her emotions felt as if they were being squished through
a meat grinder?

'We need to be married—until after the baby's born. No child of mine will grow up without my name.'

'You don't have to be married to me to give the baby your name,' Katie began. 'You can just put your name on the birth…' He pressed his finger to her lips, silencing her.

'You were happy to sleep with me for a hundred-thousand-pound investment in your company about ten minutes ago, Katherine. So why should marriage be a problem?'

'I know, but…'

'But nothing. We can separate in…' He paused. 'When is it due?'

'I won't know for sure until I've had the first scan,' she countered, beginning to feel totally overwhelmed again, and not liking it.

'Ball park,' he said.

'January.' She huffed.

'We can separate in February, then. I'll have it written into the contract.'

'What contract?' she asked, her voice rising. He was trying to railroad her. *Again.*

'The contract you're going to sign before the wedding in four weeks' time.'

'What?' She actually squeaked. He wanted to get married in a month? 'I haven't even agreed to marry you yet.'

'But you will. You know as well as I do, you're all out of options, or you wouldn't have come to me begging to prostitute yourself.'

'I didn't beg!' she gasped, outraged. 'You insisted.'

'And you agreed—then you kissed me as if your life depended on it. And we both went off like a couple of rockets on Bonfire Night, coming within one sensitive nipple of doing each other on my desk in broad daylight when any one of my employees could have walked in on us. So let's stop arguing about semantics.'

She glared at him but couldn't help but feel her panic ease a little.

At least he hadn't been faking his response any more than she had. She wasn't sure if their uncontrollable chemistry was necessarily a bonus in an already overwhelming situation. But it felt important that in at least one part of their relationship they were equally compromised.

'I need time to think about all this,' Katie murmured, suddenly unbearably weary, the emotional rollercoaster of the last twenty-four hours taking its toll as he led her back into his office.

She sat heavily in the armchair, the feeling of her life spinning out of control again doing nothing to ease her surprise when he squatted in front of her and placed warm palms on her knees.

'What is there to think about, really?' Jack murmured. 'This is a business deal which will give me what I need—a chance to elevate my social status and ensure the child is not born a bastard—and give you what you need—a chance to save your company and allow it to grow.'

He glanced at her stomach again. The muscle in his jaw tensed. Perhaps he wasn't as nonchalant about the pregnancy as he seemed. 'And give the child my financial support for the rest of its life.'

The child.

The impersonal description reverberated in Katie's skull—pragmatic and painfully dispassionate.

Her heart shrunk in her chest.

The baby really was nothing more to him than a mistake he had to rectify. Had she really believed he would feel any differently? And why would he?

She cleared her throat, trying to dislodge her sadness at the realisation her child wouldn't have a father in anything other than a financial capacity.

So what?

She didn't *want* Jack to be a father to this baby. She knew what it was like to grow up with a father who thought of you as a commodity, or a burden. Why would she wish that on her own child? She needed to deal with the practicalities now. Nothing else.

'What exactly would the marriage entail?' she managed to ask. 'Would I have to leave Wales?'

He stood up and walked to the desk. Leaning against it, he folded his arms over his broad chest as he studied her. The beard burn on her cheeks from their earlier kiss began to sting as his eyes heated with something which looked like more than just practicalities.

'Yes. You would live with me wherever I happened to be, travel with me and attend public and private events as my wife when required.' He paused, his gaze skimming her belly again. 'And your condition allows.'

'But my home and my business are in Wales.'

'You'll need to base yourself and your business in London. This is a marriage of convenience,' he said, his gaze darting to her stomach again. 'But it's not going to do the business interests we talked about much good unless it appears real. I'm afraid that's non-negotiable. I'm sure we can figure out a manageable schedule for your social responsibilities as my wife.' He frowned. 'How long has the vomiting been going on?'

She blinked, the question feeling way too personal in what—for him, anyway—appeared to be a business negotiation.

Get real, Katie, that's exactly what it is. And what you want it to be.

'Two weeks now,' she said. 'But it wasn't as bad today as it has been. I think it might finally be getting a bit better.'

His brows climbed up his forehead. '*Seri-*

ously? It's been *worse* than the exorcism routine I just witnessed?'

She let out a half-laugh, the tension in her gut easing at his horrified expression. For a split second it almost felt as if they were a real couple. But she sobered quickly, setting aside the fanciful notion. One thing she mustn't do was mistake his concern for his business priorities with any real concern for her. Or their baby. Of course he didn't want his trophy wife projectile-vomiting at inopportune moments.

'The good news is I've never been sick in the evenings,' she said. 'So social engagements shouldn't be a problem.' Of course, she usually felt exhausted by the end of the day, but he didn't need to know that yet. Hopefully the fatigue would fade too, and not having the stress of figuring out how she was going to keep her business afloat would surely help. Of course, she wasn't familiar with the kind of high-society events he was probably referring to. She would have to wing it, but she'd be damned if she'd let him know she wasn't up to the job he was offering her.

And it *was* a job. A job she was being handsomely paid for—something she would do well to remember.

He nodded. 'Good, although I doubt I'll have to make too many demands on your time. I'm not a social animal at the best of times. I'm sure we can make the marriage convincing with a few well-timed engagements…' His gaze intensified and awareness rippled over her skin. 'Especially given our extraordinary chemistry.'

Her heart bobbed into her throat and the familiar ripple shot down her spine. 'Right, about that…' Her gaze dropped away from his. 'What if I didn't want to sleep with you?'

The silence seemed to stretch out for several endless moments.

It was a lie, and she was sure he knew it. After all, she'd kissed him senseless less than ten minutes ago.

But she wasn't sure she *could* sleep with him especially while carrying his child, and not risk getting much more invested in their fake marriage than she should. Her emotions were screwy enough already.

Gee thanks, pregnancy hormones.

Sleeping with him had already had major consequences—throwing her life into complete turmoil while he seemed mostly unmoved. She didn't want to put herself at any more of a disadvantage.

He was watching her with a typically inscrutable expression but the muscle in his jaw was twitching again.

He didn't like the suggestion. But then, to her surprise, he shrugged. 'Suit yourself.'

'*Really?*'

'Of course,' he replied. 'Whatever we do together in private will be by mutual consent. That was always going to be the case. It was you who made that assumption two months ago that I would be paying you for sex.'

'Okay,' she said, feeling both chastised and embarrassed. As well as uncertain. She hadn't exactly received the concession she'd been asking for—a marriage in name only. And, given that his seduction techniques so far had turned out to be extremely effective...

Oh, for goodness' sake, Katie. Stop creating problems where there aren't any. Yet. So what if Jack Wolfe could seduce a stone? You can cross that bridge when you come to it. Time to quit while you're ahead.

Jack Wolfe was right about one thing: she was all out of options.

'So what's your answer, Katherine?' he asked, the negotiations clearly over.

She concentrated on the twitch in his jaw and controlled the familiar shot of adrenaline that was always there whenever he looked at her with that laser-sharp focus.

Take the risk. You need this—for your business and your baby. And, remember, he can't hurt you unless you let him.

'Okay,' she said. 'I guess we're getting married, Mr Wolfe.'

CHAPTER EIGHT

'I NOW PRONOUNCE YOU man and wife.'

The vicar's voice echoed in Katie's chest like the heavy clang of bells that had greeted her when she'd arrived at the historic chapel nestled in the heart of Bloomsbury ten minutes ago. She stared at her hand, weighed down by the gold band studded with diamonds Jack had eased onto her ring finger a few moments before.

Breathe, Katie, breathe.

She blinked and tried to release the air trapped in her lungs—which was starting to make her ribs ache under the bustier the stylist had insisted needed to be worn with the lavish cream silk designer wedding gown she had seen for the first time that morning.

You agreed to this, now you have to make it work. For the baby's sake.

Not easy, when she hadn't had a chance to draw a full breath since the moment she'd agreed to Jack Wolfe's devil's bargain just four weeks before.

The minute she'd said those fateful words,

Jack had taken charge. At first she'd been too shocked at the speed he'd set things into motion to really object.

He'd been unhappy at her insistence she had to return to Wales that day. Despite her exhaustion, she'd managed to stand her ground, and had felt as if she'd achieved a major concession after she'd agreed to travel home in a chauffeur-driven SUV and return to London as soon as was feasibly possible.

After a sleepless night at Cariad—spent considering and reconsidering what she'd committed to—she'd discovered the next morning that the big concession in his office had been an entirely Pyrrhic victory. A battalion of people began to arrive at the cottage in a steady stream of all-terrain vehicles.

First had come world-renowned London obstetrician Dr Patel and her team who had explained that, with Katie's permission, her pre-and ante-natal care was being transferred to the consultant's exclusive clinic in Harley Street. After a thorough check-up, and a long chat with the highly professional and wonderfully reassuring doctor—together with an assurance that Jack Wolfe would be footing the clinic's astronomical bill—Katie had swallowed her pride and agreed to switch to her care. Perhaps Jack's high-handed decision to hire the obstetrician without Katie's input didn't have to be all bad. This was his baby too, after all.

Maybe this was a small sign he was beginning to take that on board.

After Dr Patel had left, a PA called Jane Arkwright had arrived, hired to help Katie relocate her business over the next two weeks. Again, Katie had forced herself not to overreact. This was what she'd agreed to. She just hadn't thought it would happen quite this quickly. Luckily Jane was efficient and personable, and had helped to prevent Katie's anxiety hitting critical mass when she'd introduced her to a team of solicitors and accountants with a batch of documents for her to sign—including a pre-nup, a framework for what appeared to be extremely generous child support payments once the baby was born and a host of other legal and financial agreements about Wolfe Inc's investment in Cariad Cakes Etc.

Eventually, though, even Jane's capable presence couldn't stop Katie from freaking out. Why did everything have to be done in such a rush? Couldn't they postpone the wedding for a few more weeks at least?

Eventually, Katie had insisted on contacting Jack. But this time she had been unable to budge him even an inch—as his calm, measured voice had explained, everything was exactly as they had agreed. And the wedding was already booked for as soon as legally possible. Again, as they had agreed.

Yup, his decision to let her return to Cariad

had been nothing more than a clever negotiating tactic to lure her into a false sense of security before the full force of his will bowled her over like a tsunami.

And so it was two weeks later, as the afternoon light fell on the forest glade, she had locked up Cariad for the next seven months and had been directed by Jane to the all-terrain chauffeur-driven SUV for the six-hour drive to London, with the moving vans following behind.

When she'd arrived in Mayfair at midnight, though, she hadn't been driven to Jack's penthouse but to a newly purchased and luxuriously furnished six-bedroomed townhouse on Grosvenor Square with a full staff—including a personal chef, a stylist and a housekeeper—ready to cater to her every whim over the following two weeks while she 'settled into' her short-lived life as Jack Wolfe's fiancée.

Jack, though, was nowhere to be seen. Katie's relief had quickly morphed into consternation, however. After all the panic on the drive down about whether or not she would be moving into Jack's penthouse, she'd been deflated to discover her new fiancé had been *en route* to New York for a month-long trip when she'd called him two weeks ago—and that he would not be returning to London until the day of their wedding.

The days that followed had seemed to accelerate at speed through a packed schedule of visits, meetings, appointments and events all expertly curated by Jane. They'd involved everything from interviews to hire her new bakery team, to endless fittings at a designer couturier in Covent Garden to supply her with a lavish new wardrobe for the role she was about to play. She'd been too preoccupied and frankly numb to spend time dwelling on Jack's absence. And too tired each evening to do anything but fall into a dreamless sleep.

In truth, the only thing she'd still felt she had any real control over when the day of the wedding had dawned was her pregnancy. Thanks to lots of helpful advice from Dr Patel, and her insistence Katie listen to her body clock and delegate where appropriate so she got all the sleep she needed, the nausea and fatigue had begun to subside. But everything else—her new home, her new business premises in Hammersmith and the team she had begun to build—had started to feel like a strange dream she might wake up from at any time.

Somehow, her life had been so comprehensively overpowered by Jack Wolfe's organised assault on it over the past month, she'd even forgotten to stress about the prospect of her wedding until a few moments ago when she'd stepped into the chapel—to see him standing at the end of the aisle with his back to her.

As if the first sight of him again since she'd been ushered out of his office four weeks before—looking tall and indomitable in an expertly tailored wedding suit—hadn't been shocking enough, the panic she'd kept so carefully at bay during the last few days began to cinch around her ribs along with the bustier as she made her way down the aisle on the arm of his COO, Terry Maxwell.

She'd been offered the chance to invite guests but, once she'd discovered Jack was only inviting a few of his key staff, she'd declined, simply inviting Jane, who Katie had discovered was a sturdy port in the storm of her new reality.

This wasn't a real wedding. And it would have been beyond awkward to invite any of her friends, and especially Bea. After all, she could still hear her sister's gasp down the other end of the phone line when she'd told her of the marriage and the pregnancy. Bea had been her usual sweet self after the shock had worn off, and had tried to sound positive and encouraging on Katie's behalf, while Katie had been able to hear the barely disguised disbelief in her voice, wondering what had happened to her sensible sister.

Katie had channelled every acting skill she'd ever acquired to sound like a woman in love and hold back the desire to confide in her sister. Jack's legal team had insisted she sign a non-disclosure agreement preventing her from revealing the truth about the arrangement to anyone but they need not have bothered. She'd made a promise. A promise she refused to renege on.

As the vicar's words declaring the marriage complete floated up to the chapel's elegantly carved vaulted ceiling, Katie forced herself to raise her gaze from the ring.

Fierce purpose flared in Jack's eyes.

Maybe the marriage was fake, but it didn't *feel* fake as his piercing gaze proceeded to roam over her face with a possessive hunger that stole her breath.

'You may kiss the bride, Mr Wolfe,' the vicar announced with an avuncular chuckle.

Katie clutched the bespoke bouquet of Welsh woodland wild flowers—ivy, daisies and enchanted nightshade. It had been handed to her by the florist what felt like several lifetimes ago. Her gaze darted to the smiling clergyman and then back to Jack.

The sensual smile touching his lips, full of knowledge and purpose, and sent the twin tides of panic and arousal rippling through her already overwrought body.

Public displays of affection had been part of their written agreement. But, when she'd agreed to that aspect of their deception, she hadn't factored in a proper wedding with a dress, a ring and a thoughtfully designed bouquet, not to mention a ceremony in one of London's most exclusive chapels, which he'd somehow managed to pull off in less than a month.

Katie had simply assumed Jack would probably want to do something basic and understated. But, when Jane had outlined the plans for the 'big day', Katie had resigned herself to going through with it, understanding that the elaborate dog-and-pony show Jack had insisted on had to be part of the push to make the marriage seem real. So why hadn't she been better prepared for this kiss?

Her lips pursed to stop the hum of sensation getting any more pronounced as Jack's gaze lowered pointedly to her mouth. Katie's eyes fixed on his face as she tried to convey her feelings to him telepathically.

Could we please get this over with ASAP?

But Jack, being Jack, seemed in no hurry whatsoever to rush the kiss that would seal their devil's bargain.

The knowing smile spread across his features, making her sure he knew exactly how the molten weight in her belly had lodged between her thighs.

She struggled to remain calm as her breathing sawed out through congested lungs and Jack took his own sweet time lifting the jewelled veil over her head. He then spent another infinitesimal age arranging the tulle with careful precision over the hairdo a team of stylists had spent hours taming into an artful chignon threaded through with more woodland flowers.

His gaze met hers at last and his thumb skimmed down her burning cheek—possessive and electric. The contact startled her, making the fire flare at her core.

She stiffened, desperate to temper her reaction, not wanting to give him the satisfaction of knowing how easily he could turn her into a mass of pulsating sensations. But she realised she had already given him all the ammunition he needed when he leant down, his thumb sliding under her chin and sending the darts of heat shimmering south, to whisper into her ear, 'Relax, Red, I won't bite. Unless you want me to.'

Before she could think of a pithy response, his lips found hers and the last of her composure shot straight up to the vaulted ceiling.

His tongue licked across the seam. Her mouth opened, surrendering to him instinctively, just as it had done four weeks ago. The lava swelled and pulsed as he explored in expert strokes. His all-consuming kiss dragged her into a netherworld of passion and provocation as her tongue tangled with his.

And every last coherent thought flew right out of her head—bar one.

More.

Jack drove his tongue into the warm recesses of Katherine's mouth, devouring the taste he had become addicted to. A taste he'd spent the last four weeks away from his new bride to control.

The fire roared in his gut, turning his flesh to

iron as the kiss went from controlled to desperate in a heartbeat. He grasped her cheeks to angle her head and take the kiss deeper, to devour more of that glorious taste and her elemental response.

She kissed him back, her tongue duelling with his as they consumed each other in fast, greedy bites.

He heard the sound of the bouquet dropping onto stone tiles, then her hands slipped under his waistcoat, grasping fistfuls of starched linen. Her whole body shook as she clung to him, as if she were caught in a storm and he were the only thing anchoring her to earth.

His muscles tensed, the desire to scoop her into his arms and carry her to some dark, secret corner of the chapel all but unbearable.

'Mr Wolfe, perhaps you and your bride would like to sign the register?' The vicar's voice seemed to drift into his consciousness from a million miles away, through a heady fog of heat and yearning, then registered in his brain like a bombshell.

He tore his mouth from Katherine's. She was staring at him, her eyes glazed, her full lips red and swollen from the ferocity of the kiss. Her expertly arranged hair hung down on one side, tugged from its moorings by his marauding fingers.

She let go of his shirt.

How can she still drive me insane so easily?

He cleared his throat to dislodge the rock

pressed against his larynx and sucked in an unsteady breath, far too aware of the heavy erection pressing against his boxers.

It was a good thing the tailor had insisted the wedding trousers be fitted loosely or he would be giving the whole of the congregation a clear demonstration of how much he wanted his wife.

His wife.

The thought struck him for the first time that maybe this arrangement, this deal, wasn't going to be as manageable as he needed it to be. And that was without even factoring in the problem of her pregnancy.

He'd travelled all the way to New York to get a grip on his reaction to her. The fact he couldn't stop thinking about her, had even dreamed about her, had only made him more convinced distance was his best strategy, for the time being at least.

It had nearly killed him a month ago to keep his reaction to the news of her pregnancy in check. He had never planned to father a child for the simple reason he had no clue *how* to be a father, and he knew he didn't have the tools necessary to learn.

But, as he had crouched beside her in his office bathroom, the shocking discovery of her condition had been swiftly followed by another, even more disturbing, revelation.

While he didn't want to care for this child in anything other than a financial capacity, he did care for Katherine Medford. Enough to want to protect her and her business. Enough to want to mitigate the ravages of what he'd done to her body. Enough to ensure this child had his name. In the weeks since, he'd persuaded himself that the visceral reaction had to come from a need to be a better man than the man who had sired him.

Katherine had simply triggered that knee-jerk reaction with her suggestion he might try to bully her into a termination. At first he'd been furious at the whispered comment, but he'd come to accept that had to be why he had been so determined to get her to agree to this marriage. And why he had been so focussed on getting the deed done as soon as possible.

When she'd told him in his office she didn't want to sleep with him, he'd of course had an equally visceral and enraged reaction. It had taken him every single day since to get a grip on that. And realise that giving in to their sexual chemistry would be a bad move—until he was in complete control of everything else about this arrangement.

But his hard-earned control had started to slip the moment she had appeared at the back of the chapel in a swathe of seductive silk, her wild, red hair tamed beneath the wispy veil.

His breath had backed up in his lungs and he'd been… Mesmerised. Enchanted. Bewitched. And angry—with himself most of all. Because the deep yearning squeezing his ribs had reminded him of that feral kid huddled in a doorway in the West End, watching the theatregoers stroll past him on their way to the Tube—rich, clean, well-dressed, beautiful people who'd had everything, while he'd had nothing.

Katie's wedding dress should have looked classy and demure—it was what he'd requested—but the shimmering fabric had hugged Katherine's curves like a second skin, sliding sensuously over her generous hips and those high, full breasts—made even more glorious by her condition.

The evidence of her pregnancy had horrified him that day in his office, but some aspects of it now only turned him on more—which made no sense whatsoever.

She'd walked towards him—her stride bold and determined—but then he'd seen the flicker of anxiety as she reached him. It had required a titanic effort to remain aloof and in command of his senses during the endless ceremony until the vicar had finally declared them man and wife.

But, when he'd heard the invitation to kiss his bride, he'd seen the note of panic and defiance in her expression. The answering tug of posses-siveness—still tempered by the memory of that kid yearning for things he couldn't have—had made him determined to stake a claim. To prove to everyone—and Katherine most of all—she be-longed to him.

And before he'd had a chance to think better of

the impulse, he'd leaned in, inhaled a lungful of her provocative scent, seen the shocked arousal making the gold shards in her eyes gleam... And all hell had broken loose.

He'd stayed away from her precisely to avoid this uncontrolled reaction. Given their chemistry, he had no intention of having a platonic marriage, but he also had no intention of letting the hunger blindside him again, the way it had in Wales— and all those days ago in his office—until he figured out how to compartmentalise his reaction to her condition.

Distance hadn't worked, though, because his hunger for her had only become more insatiable, his desire more volatile.

Terrific.

He had a four-hour reception booked at an exclusive private members' club that he owned in Soho—entirely for the benefit of the press and his business associates.

Even better.

How the heck was he going to get through that, not to mention their first night together in the new house, without giving into this insane chemistry again?

Passion rippled through his body as he nodded to the vicar, who was watching them both with thinly disguised astonishment, his cheeks mottled with embarrassment.

'Cool, lead the way,' he said. He clasped Katherine's hand. The ring dug into his palm as he felt the tremor she couldn't disguise. He led her into the vestry to get the last of the ceremony over with. A ceremony that didn't feel nearly as pragmatic as it had when he'd originally planned it.

Katherine followed behind him, for once willing to be led without an argument. Probably because she was still as shell-shocked by that damn kiss as he was.

This hunger wouldn't last. It couldn't. But he planned to treat it with extreme caution nonetheless, because he'd never experienced a need this intense or this unstable.

Controlling it completely obviously wasn't going to happen, but no way was he unleashing this fire again until he was absolutely sure he would not get burned—any more than he had been already.

Katie struggled to hold on to the ripple of reaction as Jack's warm palm settled on her back and he leaned close to be heard over the conversations buzzing around them in the sumptuous Soho club.

'We should head back to the house,' Jack said.

It had been her first assignment as Jack Wolfe's trophy wife and she felt as if she'd done her best. She'd made pointless small talk with a host of celebrities and VIPs, got besieged by photographers shouting her name as they'd entered the venue and had managed to appear calm and collected as Jack had introduced her and they'd received a ton of champagne toasts, good wishes and inquisitive comments laced with innuendo.

The decision had been made—according to Wolfe Inc's press secretary—not to announce the pregnancy until she was showing. Katie had been pathetically grateful for that, because answering all the probing enquiries from Jack's friends and acquaintances about their whirlwind courtship had been tough enough.

She supposed she had to thank Jack for that, too. He'd more than kept up his side of the bargain, playing the solicitous bridegroom with a predatory determination which had deflected anyone who got too close. As she'd struggled to adjust to all the attention, Jack's presence by her side had made her feel strangely protected, until she'd remembered it was all an act. And, as the evening had worn on, fending off unwanted enquiries about their love affair hadn't been anywhere near as tough as stopping herself from dissolving into a puddle of need every time she'd got a whiff of his scent. Or felt the firm touch of his palm caressing her back.

Like now.

The effect he had on her had only got more intense and overwhelming as he'd remained diligently by her side through the champagne reception in the club's lavish atrium, a five-course meal of cordon bleu cuisine devised by the club's

Michelin-starred chef—which she'd barely touched—and the never-ending parade of witty and heartfelt speeches.

She stiffened as his callused fingers stroked her spine where the gown dipped, brutally aware of how addicted she had become to his clean, spicy scent. Surely that had to be the pregnancy hormones?

'Are you sure?' she whispered back, but had to stifle a yawn, the stress of the event and her struggle to keep her traitorous emotions in check—plus the fact she hadn't been able to have her usual nap this afternoon—finally taking their toll.

His lips quirked, but as his gaze raked over her the riot of sensations only intensified. How could he seem so detached? When she was burning up inside, both exhausted and on edge? Why wasn't he still struggling with the after-effects of that wedding kiss the way she was? Was her constant awareness of him *really* just the pregnancy hormones? Because the thought of going back to the house, of being alone with him again for the first time in weeks, was not helping to keep those hormones in check—especially after five solid hours of being the sole focus of his attention. Would he expect them to have a wedding night? And how was she going to resist him if he did?

He glided his thumb under her eye. 'Yes, I'm sure. You look shattered.' He glanced at her plate. 'You hardly ate a bite. Is it the nausea?'

She shook her head. 'No, it's mostly gone. I'm only sick occassionally now.'

Something she would have been a lot more grateful for if it hadn't made her even more aware of him. The morning—or rather, afternoon—sickness had once been a great way to dull this incessant attraction... Now, not a chance.

'Good,' he said, then lifted his hand to waylay one of the eager young assistants who had been hovering around them all day. 'Jenny, have the car brought round discreetly. Mrs Wolfe and I are leaving—with the minimum of fuss, if possible.'

'Yes, sir, Mr Wolfe.' The young woman, who had to be about the same age as Katie, bounced to attention so sharply Katie almost expected her to salute.

During the last few hours, she had noticed the deference with which all Jack's employees treated him, but also the fact he seemed to know all their names. She dismissed the sentimental thought, though—just because he was a good employer wasn't going to make *her* job any easier.

Despite Jack's request, it took a long twenty minutes for them to extricate themselves from the reception and the amused and ebullient well wishes of everyone from Jack's best man—an ex-rapper called Alphonse Parry who had been one of Jack's earliest business partners—to the hat-check girl, which only made Katie feel like more of a fraud.

A sleek black car was waiting at the back of the club. Jack dropped Katie's *faux* fur wrap over her shoulders while the driver opened the door.

'If you want to stay and chat, I don't mind heading back on my own,' she managed, trying to disguise the shiver which had nothing whatsoever to do with the evening breeze pebbling her skin.

He let out a wry laugh, his scarred eyebrow arching. 'Don't you think our guests might get suspicious if I let my bride go home alone on our wedding night?'

Damn. Busted.

'Oh, right—yes, of course,' she murmured, feeling like a clueless idiot.

How could she forget this was all an elaborate charade to give her child a name, keep her business afloat and allow him to…? Well, she wasn't even really sure *what* he was getting out of this, given that she definitely didn't buy the excuse he'd given her in Wales three months ago. The wedding reception had been full of some of the most important people in the global business community, every one of them falling over themselves to be nice to Jack, and her by proxy.

How could dating, or indeed marrying, a lord's daughter make him any more of a big cheese in the City of London? The fact he hadn't bothered to invite her father—thank God—surely only confirmed that?

As they settled into the car's warm interior together, the smell of new leather went some way to covering the scent of him. She had to be grateful he made no move to close the distance between them once the car pulled into traffic.

She stared out of the window, the Ritz hotel's sign reflecting off the glass as the car turned into Piccadilly. Perhaps now would be a good time to press him more on his motivations. But did she really want to know the real reason he had been so set on this marriage? Wouldn't it only complicate things further?

'You don't have to be concerned, Katherine,' he said, breaking the uncomfortable silence.

Her head whipped round as the husky timbre of his voice had the familiar ripple shooting up her spine.

He was watching her with the same intensity he had been watching her with for most of the day, ever since she'd stepped into the chapel.

She had begun to wonder during the evening if he was keeping an eye on her—ready to correct her if she said or did something to give away the real circumstances of their marriage. But there was no judgement in his gaze, only an unsettlingly direct concentration.

'We'll sleep apart tonight. Consummation of this marriage is not part of the arrangement,' he murmured.

Why not?

The thought popped out of nowhere, making the ripple sink into her sex and start to glow.

'Good to know,' she murmured, trying to sound as nonchalant as he did. And to remember she didn't want to sleep with him, because this whole situation was already disturbing enough.

His lips twisted in that disconcerting smile, but his gaze only sharpened. And she had the awful feeling he could see right through her show of indifference.

'Although on the evidence of this afternoon's kiss and the one in my office a month ago,' he continued, the relaxed tone comprehensively contradicted by that focussed gaze, which was making sensation rush over her skin like wildfire, 'I doubt we'll be able to keep our hands off each other for very long.'

'I know,' she said.

He chuckled, but the sound was as raw as she felt.

'Good to know you know that,' he said, echoing her earlier statement.

She let out an unsteady breath, the bustier so tight around her ribs she was surprised she didn't pass out. Clearly, pretending she could resist the insistent pull between them hadn't been such a smart move, because it felt as if he held all the power now that she'd been forced to admit the truth.

'So why aren't we having a wedding night?'

she challenged, trying to grab some of that power back.

His eyes widened at the direct question and she felt the instant rush of adrenaline at the realisation she'd disconcerted him. For once. Instead of the other way round.

'Is it because of the baby?' she added, when he didn't reply.

He stared, then turned away. 'No,' he said.

On the one hand, she believed him. After all, he wouldn't have kissed her with such hunger if the pregnancy had been a turn-off. But she had touched a nerve without intending to. And the questions that had been burning in the back of her mind, the ones she'd been determined not even to think about, pushed to the front.

'Do you want to talk about it?' she asked.

'Talk about what?' he asked, turning back, but the confident smile had flatlined.

No, he definitely did *not* want to talk about the pregnancy. But somehow his stubborn refusal only made her more determined to press him on it, despite her own misgivings.

They'd both been knocked off-kilter by the pregnancy. She got that. But why hadn't she questioned the hasty arrangements that he had insisted upon, and which had unnerved her so much? The speed of her relocation to London, the lavishness of today's event, the opulence of the house he'd bought for her to live in, the attentiveness with which he had treated her during the ceremony and the reception and even the mysteriously opaque motives for insisting on this marriage in the first place. Because every one of those things had disturbed her in the last month. Had he rushed her into this commitment as an elaborate way to avoid having this conversation? Maybe even to avoid thinking about it?

And, if he had, why had she fallen for it so easily? She'd told him she'd decided to have the baby, and he'd accepted it without question. But she had no idea how *he* felt about it because she hadn't asked.

'Do you want to talk about becoming a father?' she asked patiently, aware she was tiptoeing through a minefield but not able to deny her curiosity any longer. No, this wasn't just curiosity about him and the kind of father he would make. It was much more fundamental than that. She needed to know if he would ever be able to think of their child as anything other than a mistake to be rectified, a debt to be paid. And, if not, why not?

'Do I *want* to talk about it?' he mused. 'No, not particularly.'

'Why not?' she pressed, refusing to be put off again.

His gaze locked on hers, the scar on his cheek flexing. 'Because I do not intend to be a part of its life.'

The dismissive answer and the brutal, brittle tone in which he delivered it had her heart contracting in her chest. It felt like a crushing blow. Which was ridiculous, really. After all, his response only confirmed what she had already suspected.

He was being honest with her. She didn't know him well, but what she did know—that he was ruthless, driven, and uncompromising enough to buy her cooperation to further his own business ends—probably meant it was a good thing he did not want to be involved in her child's life. After all, her own father had been physically present but emotionally absent throughout her childhood, and that had somehow been worse. Surely it was better not to have a relationship with your father than to have one that was so dysfunctional it made you feel unworthy, unwanted?

But, when his gaze flicked away again, she got the sense he wasn't telling her the whole truth.

The car glided to a stop outside the Mayfair townhouse, and he remained seated while the chauffeur got out and opened her door. As she slipped out of the vehicle, she couldn't help asking, 'Are you coming inside?'

'Do you wish to consummate the marriage tonight?' he countered, the ruthless demand in his voice shaking her to the core. And putting the power firmly back in his hands, as she was sure he had intended.

'Yes… I mean, no.' She scrambled to regain the ground she'd lost. 'Oh, I have no idea.'

His harsh laugh only made her feel more confused. And more powerless. A part of her *wanted* to lose herself in the sex, to take the physical pleasure he offered so she could forget about all the things this marriage would never offer her—security, companionship, maybe even love with a man who might one day come to care for her as well as her child.

But, with her emotions so raw, she knew giving in to that urge tonight would be a very bad idea. Because she wasn't sure she could avoid the intimacy with anything like the efficiency he clearly could.

'Which is it, Mrs Wolfe?' he asked.

'No,' she said with all the conviction she could muster.

'Then I think it's best if I return to the penthouse,' he said, but he reached forward and ran his thumb down her cheek with a possessiveness that stopped her breath. 'You know where to find me, when you're ready to stop running,' he added.

She drew her head back.

He signalled the driver. After she had stepped out of the car, she watched it pull away, the traitorous desire still pulsing in her core.

As she lay in bed half an hour later, her hand curled around her stomach. She felt weary to her bones, the odd feeling of dissatisfaction joined by the terrifying thought her life had just taken an even bigger leap into the unknown.

CHAPTER NINE

'WHAT THE HELL do you mean, the Smyth-Brown board still won't let us bid on the final share allocation?' Jack shouted. He'd had yet another sleepless night alone in his penthouse. The truth was he'd been tying himself in knots ever since tying the damn knot with Katherine three days ago.

He wanted his new wife to come to him. Wanted her to admit how much she needed him so he could forget about the devastated look in her eyes when he'd been straight with her about what he planned to offer this child.

He hadn't lied about that, but the sheen of sadness in her expression still managed to get to him. It made him feel guilty about something he had never promised and could not change. Which made no damn sense whatsoever.

And now this! The main reason he'd decided to go for this marriage—well, one of the main reasons anyway—was to finally get the old fossils on the Smyth-Brown board to agree to Wolfe Inc's bid for the controlling interest of the company.

The original plan—way back when he'd first proposed to Beatrice—had been to use the marriage as leverage, to make them stop looking at him as a marauding corporate raider from the wrong side of the tracks and begin to see him as a settled family man they could trust.

His motives had become considerably more confused since then, thanks to his obsession with Beatrice's sister and the idiotic decision not to use a condom. But, if he couldn't even get this much out of the marriage, he was going to go completely insane.

'Jack, chill out,' Terry Maxwell murmured, completely unperturbed by his meltdown.

Terry was his right-hand man, his fixer, his *consigliere* and his chief financial strategist all rolled into one. Terry didn't do deference because he'd been in Jack's employ since Wolfe Inc had made its first million.

It had never bothered Jack before, but his temper surged when Terry added, 'Someone leaked the fact you're not living with your new bride. Daniel Smyth is not the only one beginning to question the authenticity of the marriage.'

'What?' Jack ground out the word, so furious and frustrated, he would not be surprised if steam began to pour out of his ears. 'Who leaked it? I want them fired immediately.'

How dared that son of a bitch question *his* integrity, especially with women, after what the guy had done to his mother?

But, before Jack could begin to work himself up into even more of a temper, Terry said, 'Jack, it could be anyone—you've been photographed coming and going from your penthouse. Perhaps the more cogent question is *why* aren't you living in Grosvenor Square with your beautiful wife?'

'That's none of your damn business,' Jack shot back, but he could hear the defensiveness in his voice as he strode to the windows of his thirty-fourth-floor office and glared at the view of the Shard on the opposite bank.

It wasn't Terry's fault he'd got into this fix with Katherine, allowing his libido and his pride to dictate his actions.

'Fair point,' Terry said, still not bothered in the least by Jack's temper tantrum. 'But, whatever your reasons, there might be a way to quash the rumours, thus fixing the problem with the Smyth-Brown takeover, while also giving the grand opening of Wolfe Maldives next month a huge publicity boost.'

Jack broke off his contemplation of the City skyline. 'Which is?' he asked, not particularly liking the sympathetic smile on his advisor's weathered face.

Terry didn't know about the true nature of his marriage, or Katherine's pregnancy, because Jack had kept all those details on a strictly need-to-know basis to stop any unwanted questions and ensure the smooth passage of the Smyth-Brown buyout. Or so he'd thought.

'The resort is already fully operational. All the staff have been hired and Wolfe Resorts' marketing division have been inviting journalists, travel bloggers and vloggers to try out the six-star experience over the last couple of weeks...' Terry began in a measured tone. 'But we can get rid of the media for a much better publicity coup.'

Jack turned round completely, to skewer his right-hand man. 'Get to the point, Terry.'

'Jack, the place is a prime honeymoon destination...' Terry stared right back at him.

'So?' Jack said, but he could already see where this suggestion was leading, because the familiar pulsing in his groin that had plagued him ever since he'd confronted Katherine on the limo ride back to the house in Mayfair on their so-called wedding night had gone into overdrive.

He had every intention of seducing his wife, and soon. He certainly didn't plan to wait much longer to settle that aspect of their relationship to his satisfaction. Especially as he knew full well her reluctance to welcome him into her bed had nothing whatsoever to do with a lack of desire. But spending any quality time with her was out. The last thing he wanted was to be subjected to another conversation like the one they'd had in the limo.

He hadn't married her to have an actual relationship with her. That had been the whole point of contracting her to *pose* as his wife—which she seemed to have conveniently missed. Of course, the pregnancy complicated that somewhat. But he didn't talk about his past, or his motives or feelings, with anyone. And certainly not with women he was sleeping with… Or intended to sleep with. Especially when they had the unique ability to blindside him with lust—the way Katherine did—and were also carrying his child.

'Jack, don't be deliberately obtuse,' Terry said, looking pained now. 'You've just got married. Wolfe Maldives isn't due to open for another month. A two-week honeymoon there with your blushing bride would garner the kind of organic global media reach your PR department would have wet dreams about for years.'

No way in hell.

That was what his head shouted but, even as he opened his mouth to tell Terry to forget it, the image of Katherine in a skimpy bikini, strolling out of the lagoon's glittering blue waters, those generous breasts bouncing enticingly as she moved, blasted out of his subconscious and sunk deep into his abdomen.

Damn.

He closed his mouth. And frowned.

As much as he hated to admit it, Terry had a point. The truth was, he didn't give a damn about the golden PR opportunity. But the chance to have Katherine all to himself—where he could seduce her in private—held some obvious advantages. Surely he'd already done enough to disabuse her of any sentimental notions she might have had about this marriage?

'Two weeks is too long,' he said, his voice dropping several octaves as more images of Katherine—wet and willing in a luxury beach setting—began to galvanise his resolve. 'I can't afford to spend that much time away from the business.' Which wasn't a lie.

Having Katherine all to himself in paradise—and making every one of the prurient fantasies he'd had about her since their first merry meeting come true—was appealing to all his baser instincts. But he wasn't about to push his luck.

'Really?' Terry looked sceptical. 'You haven't taken a proper holiday in the ten years I've known you.'

'I'm a workaholic, Terry. I like working. I can't spend a fortnight twiddling my thumbs just for a good photo op.' Not that he planned to be twiddling *his* thumbs, exactly.

Terry sent him a garrulous look. 'How about ten days, then?'

'A week,' Jack countered. 'We'll leave tomorrow night,' he added, the adrenaline rush surging at the thought he would only have to endure one more night—two at the most—without Katherine in his bed. 'In the Wolfe jet.'

He sat behind his desk, feeling more settled than he had in days. Hell, weeks. Make that four months ago. Ever since the first time he'd set eyes on his future trophy wife in her Little Red Riding Hooker outfit. He smiled. Maybe he could get her to bring it so he could peel it off her, the way he'd dreamed of doing ever since that night.

'That's great, Jack.' Terry rubbed his hands together with undisguised glee. 'I'll talk to Sully in the marketing division and the resort management team. And I'll let Gorinda know so she can rearrange your schedule. Do you want her to inform Mrs Wolfe of your plans?'

He looked up from his desk. 'Nah, I'll speak to her myself,' he said as the surge of adrenaline took on a fiercely possessive edge. 'Tell Gorinda I'll be eating in Grosvenor Square tonight.'

It was way past time he started laying down the law in this marriage—which was supposed to be for *his* convenience, not hers. He'd paid handsomely for the damn privilege after all. He'd been considerate—mindful of her delicate condition and the huge changes he was imposing on her life and her business. But she'd said herself at the reception that the sickness wasn't a big problem any more. He knew from his business manager's report that Cariad Cakes was now firmly established in its new premises in Hammersmith, and he had seen the way she'd looked at him on their wedding night. She was as hungry for him as he was for her. And he'd given her three long days and nights to come to terms with the way things were, which was more than long enough.

CHAPTER TEN

'JACK, YOU'RE HERE!' Katie stopped dead at the entrance to the dining room, a mix of shock and panic and exhilaration duelling in her chest at the sight of her husband sitting at the table where she'd eaten alone for the last three nights.

His white business shirt was open at the neck to reveal a hint of the tattoo across his chest, the sleeves rolled up tanned, muscular forearms, his hair mussed and his jaw darkened with a day's beard. The scene should have felt at least a little bit domestic. But it didn't. The possessive glint in his eyes echoed in her abdomen.

Yeah, right. Jack Wolfe is about as domesticated as his namesake.

'And you're late,' he said as his penetrating gaze glided over her flour-stained clothing and the weary set of her shoulders. 'You're working too hard.'

'Well, there's a lot to do,' Katie said a little defensively, disconcerted by the note of concern and the fact it made her feel cherished when she knew it wasn't real. 'I would have left earlier, though, if I'd known you were joining me for dinner…' she said, trying at least to *sound* like a dutiful wife. After all, it was what they'd agreed on. Although, she hadn't felt like a wife in the three days since their wedding. He hadn't even contacted her.

At first, she had fretted she'd somehow offended him by being honest with him and not inviting him into her bed. His comment about the baby had upset her, making her feel uniquely vulnerable, but not seeing or hearing from him for three days had only made the unsettled feeling worse…not that it was exactly calm at the moment.

How did he manage to throw her for a loop simply by breathing?

'I didn't expect to see you tonight,' she added rather inanely as he picked up one of the freshly baked bread rolls laid out on the table by the kitchen staff.

'Last time I looked, this was my house,' he said as he buttered the roll, watching her intently as she walked to the place setting at the other end of the table.

'Are you planning to move in, then?' she asked, not entirely sure how she felt about the prospect. The twin tides of panic and exhilaration now danced a jig in her chest, and a few other places besides.

She couldn't avoid him for ever, and she really didn't want to. Surely getting to know him better had to be a good thing? Especially as she'd come to the conclusion—after three days of overthinking what he'd said about fatherhood—that perhaps she just needed to be patient with him.

He'd said he didn't intend to play a part in the baby's life. But maybe that would change. The pregnancy had to have been a major shock for him too—however good he was at hiding it. And he didn't have the same physical connection with their grain-o'-rice as she did. Of course, the baby would seem like a totally abstract concept to him at this point.

'Not tonight,' he said as a waiter arrived with the first course.

The exhilaration dimmed a bit as a beautifully prepared salad made up of crisp romaine lettuce, finely sliced radishes, carrots, apple and endives, and drizzled with a creamy dressing, was placed in front of her.

'Oh… Okay,' she said, trying to hide her disappointment. She tucked into the salad. Her appetite had returned full force in the last few weeks, despite all the tension over her situation with Jack but, as she wracked her brains to figure out what he was doing here, she couldn't swallow a bite.

'We're heading to the Maldives tomorrow

night for a week,' he said. 'So you'll need to brief your team at the bakery and have the housekeeper arrange your packing.'

Katie dropped her fork onto the plate, so shocked by her new husband's bland pronouncement, she barely noticed the splatter of salad dressing hitting the table cloth. *'What?'*

He let out a gruff laugh, but his gaze remained locked on hers, more provocative than humorous. 'I believe it's the usual protocol after a wedding to have a honeymoon.'

'Except this isn't a usual wedding, is it?' she said. 'I haven't even heard from you in three days.'

He placed his knife and fork on the plate, before trapping her again in that blazing blue gaze. 'Have you missed me, Mrs Wolfe?'

Yes, you stupid...

She quashed the unhelpful thought before it could burst out of her mouth and give him even more power.

'I'm just saying, this isn't a normal marriage.'

He picked up his cutlery again, speaking in a conversational tone as he sliced through an endive leaf. 'Perhaps not, but I thought you understood the marriage has to appear to be real.'

'But... There was nothing about a honeymoon in the contract,' she floundered. She didn't want to go on some romantic getaway with him—for a whole week—even if it was only for the sake of appearances. She was having enough trouble sitting across the dining room from him without getting fixated on the way his shoulders strained the seams of his shirt, or recalling the rigid, resistant look on his face when she had asked him about his thoughts on fatherhood.

Getting to know him slowly, and carefully, with a full staff in attendance was one thing. Surviving a week of his focussed attention while battling her own insecurities was quite another. How would she be able to deny the insistent need with him right there? Sleeping with him would fundamentally change the parameters of their agreement in a way that could be dangerous if she wasn't emotionally prepared for the change.

'If you read the small print, it stated you would be required to travel with me,' he continued in that forceful, pragmatic tone that got on her nerves. 'This honeymoon is part of that commitment. You signed it, Red. Are you trying to renege on the deal already?'

'No, but…' She gathered her ragged breathing, forcing herself to remain calm. She'd known he would be dominant, demanding. She'd expected that. She must not lose her temper, because that would just give him the upper hand, especially as she was beginning to think he enjoyed provoking her.

'You said we could negotiate our work schedules. I can't very well leave my business for a week with less than a day's notice.'

He glanced at his watch. 'Our flight isn't leaving until eight tomorrow night, so you've got most of the day to brief your team.'

'Fine, but it's still too soon to relinquish—'

'There's an excellent Internet connection where we're going.' He cut her off, the prickle of impatience sending an answering prickle of irritation through her. 'You'll be able to check in with your team if necessary.'

Standing, he dropped his napkin on the table.

'But this isn't fair,' she said, annoyed when she heard the whiney tone of her own voice. 'I don't *want* to go to the Maldives.'

With you. Alone. On a fake honeymoon. Which will mean nothing to you and might mean something to me.

He strode towards her and tucked a knuckle under her chin to brush his thumb over her bottom lip.

She jerked her head back, but it was already too late. He had to have seen the awareness flare at the brief touch.

He planted his hands in his pockets, the smile as smug as it was predatory. 'I understand very well, Red. You think by avoiding each other this incessant heat will just go away. It won't.'

'But what if I'm not ready?'

His scarred eyebrow lifted, his cast-iron confidence completely undimmed by her declaration.

Damn him.

'I told you anything we do in private would be your choice. That hasn't changed.'

'Then why are you insisting on going to—?'

'However...' He interrupted her. *Again!* 'I did not agree to pretend the heat between us doesn't exist. Personally, I believe enjoying it for as long as your condition allows will make this marriage a lot more pleasurable for both of us. And trying to avoid it will only increase the problem. So I guess the battle lines are drawn.'

The tell-tale weight sunk into her sex as he returned to his seat and finished his salad. She sucked in a breath, too furious to speak.

Of all the arrogant, high-handed, conceited, overbearing...

She picked up her knife and fork again, ignoring the tremble in her fingers. Fine, she'd go on his stupid honeymoon and show him he couldn't bend her to his will. But she'd refuse to be bulldozed back into his bed... By his hungry kisses, his addictive scent or that seductive promise in his cool blue eyes...even if it killed her.

Although it very well might.

After a frantic day spent running through recipes, answering countless emails, checking orders and getting her new business manager up to speed on all the commitments she was being forced to cancel for the next week, Katie was holding on to her indignation by a thread when her car arrived at Heathrow the following evening.

Instead of being dropped off in Departures, though, they were met by a passport official before being whisked through the airport, the lights of incoming planes shining in the night sky overhead. The car drove past the airport buildings to arrive at a huge private hangar behind one of the runways. A sleek silver jet took up all the available space as the car parked beside the metal steps.

She swallowed heavily as the driver opened her door then began unloading the luggage the staff must have packed earlier that day—*three* suitcases worth of luggage containing clothes she had never seen.

She frowned. Up until now, she'd really been far too preoccupied with the pregnancy, the wedding, the huge changes to her business and her constant panic about how to navigate the deal she'd made with Jack without losing her mind to think too much about the world of luxury she had entered. A world she'd been excluded from ever since she was a teenager. A world she'd left without a backwards glance.

But, as she climbed the steps into the jet, it occurred to her Jack Wolfe's lavish luxurious world was way, *way* more exclusive than her father's. She'd come from money and, although she'd never enjoyed the strings attached when she'd lived under her father's control, she knew how this world worked. Or at least, she had thought she did. But, even as the daughter of a British lord, she'd never travelled on a private plane—or had a passport official give her a personal service. Or had three huge suitcases full of clothes she'd never worn packed for her by someone else for a week-long holiday.

Except it's not a holiday, it's a honeymoon.

She puffed out her cheeks, the frustration that had been building ever since Jack's high-handed demand yesterday at dinner giving way to something a lot less fortifying and more disturbing.

She'd barely had time to think in the past month. Perhaps that was why it hadn't really occurred to her until this moment that *everything* about her new life with Jack Wolfe was way outside her comfort zone.

As she stepped into the plane's interior, she was greeted by a hostess uniformed in the red and black colours of the Wolfe Inc logo. The middle-aged woman smiled and took her coat, before directing her to the plane's interior.

'Mr Wolfe is seated in the lounge area, waiting for you, Mrs Wolfe,' she said.

Mrs Wolfe.

She'd been addressed by her married name

several times since the wedding. But it had all seemed like an elaborate act until now. A knot formed in her stomach to go with the one in her throat.

She nodded, suddenly feeling woefully underdressed in the worn jeans and plaid shirt combo she had been wearing all day to direct traffic in Cariad Cakes' industrial kitchen.

Jack sat in one of the large cream leather armchairs in the plane's lounge, typing something on his phone. The cabin was darker than she had expected, the lighting no doubt subdued for take-off. A single spotlight turned his short dark hair to a gleaming ebony and cast his handsome features into stark relief. He hadn't shaved all day, and the beginnings of the beard shadowing his jaw, together with the scarred eyebrow, made him look even more rugged and untamed than usual, despite the sharply tailored suit trousers and ubiquitous white shirt perfectly fitted to his muscular torso.

'Mrs Wolfe has arrived, sir,' the hostess announced behind her.

Jack's blue gaze locked on her face as he clicked off the phone. 'Good evening, Mrs Wolfe,' he said, the polite greeting loaded with a meaning that felt anything but polite thanks to the feral gleam in his eyes and the husky timbre of his voice.

She'd expected him to have his army of assistants with him on the flight but, as the hostess excused herself to prepare for take-off, Katie realised they were alone.

'Hi,' she said, but the word came out on a high-pitched squeak. Mortified, she cleared her throat of the rubble gathered there, and tried again. 'Hello, Jack.'

'Glad to see you made it in time for take-off,' he said, the slight edge suggesting he hadn't appreciated being kept waiting.

She hadn't arrived with only minutes to spare deliberately—she'd been extremely busy all day—but his tone still rankled.

'Did I have a choice?' she snapped.

A sensual smile—part arrogance, part amusement and yet full of approval—had her heartbeat leaping in her chest. She *knew* he enjoyed provoking her. But why hadn't she realised until now how much more he enjoyed it when she rose to the bait?

He chuckled. 'I can't very well go on a honeymoon on my own, now, can I?' he said, the mocking twinkle in his eyes making him look even more attractive.

The bastard.

Oddly—given her anxiety about what exactly they were going to be doing in the Maldives, and her indignation at the high-handed way he'd sprung this trip—she found her own lips twitching.

'I suppose not,' she conceded as she took the seat opposite him. She sunk into the soft, buttery leather, suddenly aware of how exhausted she was. The extreme fatigue of her early pregnancy had been replaced by a more manageable tiredness in the last few weeks, but she'd been on her feet most of the day—and coping with the inevitable sexual tension of being in Jack Wolfe's orbit didn't help.

'Although you may wish you had after a week stuck with me spinning my wheels,' she offered. 'I don't think I'm the "lying on the beach" type.'

It wasn't a lie. She couldn't remember the last time she'd taken a break, let alone been able to afford a holiday. She'd been working two or three jobs at a time ever since she'd left home—and even before leaving home she'd had a secret Saturday job because she'd wanted to be as financially independent as possible from her father.

'Neither am I,' Jack murmured. The approval in his gaze became hot and fluid, causing awareness to sizzle over her skin. 'I guess we'll have to find a way to keep each other occupied.'

The sizzle flared across her collarbone and rose into her cheeks.

His gaze narrowed on her burning face and the knowing smile widened.

If only she could conjure up a smart, pithy comeback, but it would have been next to impossible to fake indifference, even if she hadn't been dead on feet.

The pilot's voice rang out over the intercom to inform them they had just been given a departure slot and would be taking off in ten minutes.

Katie fastened her seat belt as instructed and glanced out of the window, realising the plane was already moving and had left the bright interior of the hangar. The lights of the terminal building as they passed it illuminated the congested lines of passengers waiting impatiently at their departure gates.

She sighed and rolled her head back, only to get trapped once again in Jack's watchful gaze. But the sizzle dropped to a distant hum as fatigue settled over her like a warm blanket.

Her mouth cracked open in a huge yawn. 'Good to know there's at least one advantage to having a gazillionaire for my fake husband.'

His right eyebrow rose, drawing her attention to the scar, which had begun to mesmerise her. Curiosity and sympathy joined the potent hum of arousal.

Who *had* given him that scar? It must have hurt so much.

'Which is…?' he asked, the smile gone.

'No boarding queues,' she murmured, then shifted round in her seat away from that disturbing all-seeing gaze. Yawning again, she slipped off

her shoes, snuggled her head into the soft leather
and tucked her aching feet under her bottom.

She blinked at the red lights on the plane's
wing tip flashing as they swung towards the runway. The jet engine's powerful rumble seemed
to amplify the insistent hum in her abdomen but,
as the plane accelerated down the runway, she
couldn't seem to keep her eyes open. Eventually
the flashing light dragged her into the darkness
and she let herself fall under its spell.

Jack stared at his wife as the jet lifted into the
night sky, not sure whether to be bemused or
beguiled by the sight of her curled on the seat
opposite, fast asleep.

Her russet hair haloed around her head, tendrils escaping from the practical ponytail to curl
down her neck. Chocolate stains covered her
well-worn jeans and the green and brown plaid
shirt. She looked like a lush tomboy, the light
flush on her freckle-dusted skin only adding to
the spike in his groin. A few buttons had come
undone on her shirt, giving him a tantalising
glimpse of her cleavage as she slumbered, her
body contorted into what looked like a very uncomfortable position.

She had been exhausted when she arrived.
He had seen it in the smudges under her eyes
and the lipstick that had been chewed off her

lips hours ago. The stab of guilt joined the ache in his groin.

He shifted in his seat, visions of her soft, satiny flesh, that rich spicy scent of salted caramel, ripe apples and wild flowers permeating the cabin.

His gaze dipped and he imagined easing open the other buttons on her shirt, nuzzling the soft fragrant skin of her cleavage as it was revealed inch by tantalising inch, kissing the pulse in her collarbone, unhooking her bra, lifting her breasts free and sucking the plump pink nipples until they hardened against his...

He swore softly and swung his head away from her slumbering form to glare out of the aircraft's window. He gripped the arm rests as the inevitable wave of heat swelled. He sucked in a tortured breath. When had he ever been tormented to this extent by any woman? It was becoming ridiculous. Not to mention distracting.

Christ, if she knew the hold she had on him she would surely exploit it.

The carpet of city lights below them disappeared as the jet headed into cloud cover and began to level off at its cruising altitude.

The hostess appeared. 'Mr Wolfe, the bed chamber is ready for you and your wife,' she said, sending him a rather too amused smile.

'Right, thanks,' he murmured. 'If you could leave us, please.'

The woman immediately got the message and left.

He reached for his laptop, planning to work until Katherine awoke. But, as the minutes ticked past, he found it impossible to concentrate on the bids being put in place for the Smyth-Brown shares, something which should have had all his attention.

He sighed and closed the laptop. Hell, he'd have to check the contracts another day. It would be several months yet before the takeover was finalised and he could finally get his revenge on the man who had discarded his mother.

He had time.

His fervour for the fight would come back as soon as his new wife had become less of a distraction. Sun, sea, sand and lots of mind-blowing sex would cure this strange *ennui*.

His gaze landed back on Katherine, who had contorted herself into another uncomfortable-looking shape. He could smell her. The tantalising earthy aroma sent another unwelcome surge of arousal through his system.

She huffed and shifted, drawing her knees up and her chin down to snuggle tighter into the seat's headrest, almost as if trying to protect herself from something. Her eyelids flickered with dreams, her brows furrowed and her lips pursed into a tight line, her breathing becoming rapid suggesting, whatever the dreams were, they weren't happy or benign.

The shaft of guilt hit more forcefully. He dismissed it. She looked healthier than she had when she'd come to his office and told him of the pregnancy. A week in paradise would be good for her.

He tilted his head to one side to study her, while ignoring the tightness in his chest at the thought of what might be causing her unpleasant dreams.

Surely her nightmares had to be due to the uncomfortable position she was trying to sleep in? Nothing more disturbing than that. Even though it would be torture for him, she was clearly too tired for them to satisfy this hunger tonight.

He undid his seatbelt and approached her. Clasping her shoulder, he rocked her gently. 'Katherine, wake up and I'll show you to the bedroom.'

When she didn't stir, he tried again.

She shook her head, moaned and turned away from him.

'Damn,' he whispered. She really was shattered.

Unclipping her seatbelt, which had become tangled around her hips, he hooked one arm under her bent knees, the other across her back and scooped her up against his chest.

Her cheek nestled against his collarbone, her body soft and pliant and satisfyingly substantial in his arms, her warm breath tickling the skin under his chin. Heat gathered and throbbed in eddying waves in his groin, adding to the torture as he carried her through the darkened cabin and opened the narrow door to the master bedroom.

The hostess had turned down the bed, and a night light embedded in the headboard had been switched on, casting an eerie glow. But, as Jack deposited his cargo in the middle of the smooth satin comforter, Katherine's eyelids fluttered open. Trapped in her emerald gaze, her pupils dark and unfocussed, his breath squeezed his lungs. And his heart hammered against his ribs in hard, heavy thuds.

Thoughts of taking advantage of her drowsy, semi-conscious state bombarded his tortured body. He imagined joining her on the bed, stripping off her clothing, undoing his trousers to free the strident erection and thrusting heavily into the tight, wet heat.

But then her hand reached up to cradle the taut muscle in his cheek, the gentle touch soothing the rampant thoughts—as if he were a wild beast and she a fairy-tale maiden come to rescue him from his own depravity. Before he had a chance to make sense of the ludicrous notion, her fingertip stroked the jagged scar.

His heartbeat slowed, every part of his being focussed on that consoling, feather-light caress, and for one terrifying moment he almost believed it would cure the pain of his past.

'Does it still hurt?' she asked, her voice thick with sleep, her faced softened by the dream-like quality of someone who was not fully aware of what they were saying or doing.

He shook his head, but the relentless, insistent desire shifted, swept along by something a great deal more disturbing... Longing.

'Who did it?' she asked, still caressing the torn, ugly flesh, the symbol of how defenceless he'd once been.

'The man I thought was my father,' Jack said as the truth released from his chest in a guttural whisper.

Anguish shadowed her eyes, the glint of moisture reflecting in the half-light and making him aware of the gold flecks in the emerald-green. But then she blinked and a single tear dripped from the corner of her eye to roll down the side of her face. 'I hate him,' she said.

Shock washed through him like acid as his heart clamoured and roared, the desire returning in a heady rush but driven this time by the brutal yearning.

He grasped her consoling fingers and dragged them away from the ruined flesh. He levered himself off the bed. Her gaze remained riveted to his, conveying emotions he didn't want to see, didn't even want to acknowledge, but could feel turning the weight in his chest into a ten-ton slab of reinforced concrete. 'Go back to sleep, Katherine. I'll see you in the morning.'

He left the room, closed the door behind him and headed into the other bedroom. Not caring any more about the torturous desire still throbbing in his groin.

Because he had a much bigger problem to deal with now. How the hell was he going to lift this concrete slab off his chest while spending a week in paradise with the woman who had dumped it there in the first place?

CHAPTER ELEVEN

KATIE SHIELDED HER EYES against the early-morning sunlight glittering on the turquoise blue of the lagoon. A lagoon which stretched for miles towards the horizon in every direction—literally a vision of paradise.

A salt-scented breeze moved through the palm trees that fringed the beach, adding a hushed rustle to the tranquil day. The translucent sea lapped against the shoreline in desultory waves. Standing on the bedroom terrace of the stunning steel-and-glass structure that was Jack's house on the island, she wondered where her so-called husband was.

Is he avoiding me?

She'd awoken yesterday, after eleven hours virtually comatose, when the private jet had touched down in Malé at midday. She and Jack had been driven by limousine from the airport through the colonial town to the port, where a motor launch had waited to whisk them across the water towards the Ari Atoll and Wolfe Maldives' private island.

One thing she remembered clearly was waking up in the plane's bedroom, alone, strange dreams still intruding on her consciousness—of Jack, his face tense, cautious and wary, shock and brutal sadness clouding his eyes. Even now, twenty-four hours later, she could still feel the texture of his scar against her fingertips, the warm skin ridged and torn. She gripped the balcony railing. Had she touched him in her sleep? Had he carried her into the plane's bedroom?

The man I thought was my father.

His gruff whisper murmured through her memory, as it had so many times on their strangely stilted journey from the airport to the island, and during the afternoon and evening she'd spent alone in the house after he had disappeared with some excuse about having to work.

Had he *actually* confided in her? The words had been full of bitterness but tinged with vulnerability—as if his answer had been wrenched from his very soul. Or had she imagined the dream-like encounter on the flight?

She had considered asking him about it during the limousine transfer to the port in Malé and the breathtaking journey on the motor launch across the vast blue sea. But he had been preoccupied ever since they'd left the airport, either talking on his phone, reading contracts or tapping out messages on his laptop. In fact, she'd barely exchanged two words with him since she'd walked into the jet's lounge area, feeling well-rested but still confused and on edge, to find him waiting for her, his watchful gaze holding so many secrets.

He'd been tense, brooding, the withdrawn quality telling her louder than words to keep her distance. And, even though she had decided any intimacy between them would be dangerous, she had missed the mocking, dominating—and impossibly hot—man who had invited her on this trip in the first place.

When they'd arrived at Wolfe Maldives—which had appeared like a tropical oasis in the midst of the never-ending blue, the main building a white wood-framed colonial palace which blended into the palm trees—Jack had disappeared with a team of his assistants and the resort's managerial staff.

So this was going to be a working honeymoon, then? Funny he hadn't mentioned that when she'd been freaking out about it at dinner three nights ago.

After he'd left her, she had ignored the pang of regret and concentrated on the tour she was given of the stunning facilities: two swimming pools, a fully equipped gym and several different dining areas, including one on a floating platform in the lagoon, draped in white linen that billowed in the breeze. There were tennis courts, a spa and a seasports area equipped with everything from jet-skis to paddle boards and snorkelling equipment, plus a dive hut where a diving instructor had offered to introduce her to the wonders of the reef that surrounded the island during her stay.

Then she'd been driven in a golf buggy to the Owner's Cottage on the other side of the island. Whoever had named it a cottage had clearly been delusional. Cariad was a cottage. The two-storey stone and glass structure perched on the edge of a white sand cove was nothing short of a palace.

After exploring the five-bedroom house and its grounds while the staff unpacked their luggage, she had been served a three-course meal on the veranda by the charmingly discreet staff...while Jack had been conspicuous by his absence.

After watching the sinking sun create a sensational light show of pinks and oranges and flaming reds from the jetty, she'd headed to bed, feeling anxious but also lonely.

Where was he?

Did Jack plan to join her in the master bedroom tonight? How would she feel if he woke her? Should she have stayed up to greet him when he finished his work commitments? What was her role here? Because she had no idea.

But, when she'd woken this morning, the bed beside her had been empty. And, after she'd checked the property to find another one of the bedrooms slept in but still no sign of Jack, the bewilderment and loneliness turned to agitation.

She frowned, the stunning, sun-drenched scen-

ery doing nothing to dispel the knots in her belly
that had been forming since yesterday.

Now she knew a little of how Mrs Rochester
must have felt—the unwanted bride hidden away
and going insane in the attic. Albeit this was a
luxury paradise attic where every possible ame-
nity waited to distract her from the fact her new
husband wanted to have nothing to do with her...

Not that they were a *real* husband and wife,
she told herself staunchly, but still it felt as if
she'd been brought to the Maldives under false
pretences. What had become of the man who'd
teased and tormented her, who had insisted the
heat between them needed to be dealt with? And
what exactly was she supposed to do about the fact
she was starting to want it dealt with too?

She breathed in the clean, salty air, the sun
warming her skin. Was it possible that what had
happened in the plane's bedroom hadn't been a
dream? Was it behind his disappearing act? Was
Jack running scared now?

And, if he was, what did she want to do about
it?

*Find him. Because avoidance clearly isn't
working. It's just making me more insane.*

They had six more days together in paradise
and six months until the baby was born. She was
tired of running—not just from the insistent desire, but the strange connection they seemed to
share. She needed to discover if what he'd told her

about the scar was true. Because that furious jolt of compassion for him, and the brutalised boy he'd been, was still there throbbing under her breast bone like an open wound.

Maybe the sensible thing would be to forget about what she thought he'd said to her. It would be horribly embarrassing if she'd conjured the whole scenario up from some desperate desire buried deep in her psyche. Always a possibility.

But she'd never been sensible when it came to relationships. She'd always been reckless, impulsive and passionate. It was how she'd survived on her own for years, especially after her grandmother's death. Why she'd been in Jack Wolfe's penthouse that night at her sister's request. And probably one of the reasons why she had agreed to this marriage in the first place.

Her decision to sign on Jack's dotted line had never been as simple or straightforward as she'd wanted to believe—it hadn't just been about the unplanned pregnancy or her desperation to get out from a mountain of debt and turn her business into a going concern. It had also been about that fierce, intense desire in Jack's eyes whenever he looked at her and the strange sense that he saw her in a way no other man ever had.

Maybe that intense yearning was simply about sex for him, but it was about more than that for her. And it was time she acknowledged it and found a way forward.

Striding back into the bedroom, she donned one of the designer swimsuits that had been brought for her. The one-piece had a fifties vibe, cut high on the leg with a criss-cross design across her chest that lifted her breasts, while the vibrant letter-box-red matched the russet tones of her hair. Although the costume didn't show as much flesh as the bikinis, it flattered her hour-glass shape and gave her a confidence she needed.

She tied up the unruly locks of her hair in a casual knot, slathered all the places she could reach in sun lotion then added a pair of denim cut-offs, some beach sandals and a lose-fitting white linen shirt to her ensemble. She wasn't about to throw herself at the man if he didn't want her. But she refused to allow him to dictate all the terms of their marriage. He'd dictated enough already.

After downing a cup of mint tea and a bowl of the home-baked granola and fresh fruit laid out by the invisible staff on the stunning black quartz breakfast bar, she headed out onto the stone pool-terrace.

She squinted into the sunshine. It had to be getting close to ten o'clock. She'd been up for over an hour and Jack was still nowhere in sight.

He's definitely avoiding me.

Her heartbeat ticked into her throat, her breathing the only sound as silence greeted her.

A pair of sandy deck shoes had been left beside one of the loungers. *Bingo.*

The oval pool sparkled in the sunlight, fringed by large planters of exotic tropical flowers and shrubs. On one side of the beach beyond was the wooden jetty from where she had watched the sunset the night before, a gleaming motor launch and a couple of jet-skis docked at the end. As she scanned the cove, her gaze caught on a glimmer of movement about a mile out, coming around the point on the other side of the bay.

She shielded her eyes. Was that a dolphin?

But as the sleek shape drew closer she recognised it as a man swimming, or rather powering, across the lagoon in fast, efficient strokes, his dark hair and tanned skin contrasting sharply with the bright, translucent turquoise of the sea.

Jack! My invisible husband.

The knots in her stomach grew, and her thigh muscles quivered as he strode out of the water and onto the beach below the terrace. Dragging off a pair of goggles, he picked up a towel left on the sand and scrubbed himself dry in brusque strokes.

She stepped back into the shade of one of the flowering scrubs, the knots in her stomach tightening.

His muscular arms and wide shoulders glistened in the sunshine, the wet swimming shorts clinging to his thighs and hanging from his lean waist, displaying the ridge of his hip flexors. After rubbing the towel through the short strands of hair, he dragged off the shorts.

The last of her confusion and irritation dried in her throat, turning to something that felt uncomfortably like shock... And awe. It was the first time she'd seen him naked since he had disrobed in the grey, shadowy light of Cariad's storm-tossed bedroom.

Even though he stood a good twenty feet away, the bright sunshine made the view a lot clearer. The tickle of panic in the back of her throat—at the spectacular sight of Jack Wolfe stark-naked—was nothing compared to the flood of sensation working its way up her torso as she took her time devouring every detail—the tan demarcation line on his hip, the bush of black hair framing the long column of his sex before he hooked the towel around his waist.

Apparently Jack worked out... A lot. Something she hadn't registered the last time she'd seen him naked in the furore of need. During her lonely granola breakfast, Katie had rehearsed a script of all the things she wanted to say to Jack when she finally located him. But as he groped around on the sand, then picked up a pair of spectacles, every last word of those imagined opening gambits were whipped away on the breeze along with the last of her temper. And all that was left was the knot in her throat, the sultry insistent ache in her abdomen and the clatter of her heart beating against her ribs.

Jack wore glasses. How had she not known that?

As he headed towards the house with his head down, running his fingers through the cropped hair, she had a sudden vivid memory of the night they'd met and his unfocussed gaze as he'd glared at her. How myopic was he? Because it had seemed for a minute as if he'd had to use touch to locate his spectacles.

As he drew close, she stepped out from behind the plant.

Show time.

His head rose and he stopped dead. Tension rippled through his body, but even behind the lenses of his glasses—which had darkened in the sun— she could see something fierce yet guarded flash across his face. Surprise and desire, certainly, but also a wary alertness.

And suddenly the last of her doubts disappeared. He *had* said those words to her about the scar in the jet two nights ago. It hadn't been a dream. Was that why he had been avoiding her?

Compassion blindsided her.

'Katherine,' he murmured, managing to temper his reaction sooner than she could. 'You're awake?' He sounded surprised as his possessive gaze took in everything, from her scarlet toenails in the open sandals to the damp tendrils sticking to her neck.

'I've been up for an hour,' she said, determined not to get sidetracked by the hum in her abdomen or the electrifying awareness that pulsed around them.

'Why didn't you come back last night?' she asked.

'I did,' he said, deliberately misinterpreting her question. 'You were asleep.'

'Don't lie.' She crossed her arms over her chest. 'You've been avoiding me, Jack. Why?'

'Because I've been busy.' Jack ground out the words, struggling to keep his voice firm and even when everything inside him was clamouring to touch her, to taste her, to scoop her into his arms, tear off the shorts that barely covered her butt, tug down the swimsuit peeking out from beneath her shirt and fill his mouth with the taste of salt and apples on her breasts.

Hell, how could he still want her so much after swimming for miles and burying himself in work yesterday to keep the hell away from her? Shouldn't this hunger have faded by now, or at least become a lot more manageable? Especially as she knew things about him now he didn't want anyone to know.

When they had arrived yesterday, he'd only planned to stay away from her for an hour or two, but the yearning had only become more insistent as the afternoon had worn on.

He needed to be able to control it, or he might blurt out something else. And he already hated that she'd caught him without his lenses in. The heavy glasses always made him feel weak, reminding him of the child he'd been, trying to dodge fists he couldn't see.

'Doing what?' she asked.

'Surely you can't be bored already?' he countered, damned if he was going to answer any more of her questions.

'We're supposed to be here on our honeymoon, Jack,' she countered right back. 'Don't you think the staff will find it odd if all you do while we're here is work…?' Her gaze dipped. 'And swim.'

Of course they did. He'd seen the confusion on the resort manager's face when he'd insisted on spending all afternoon and evening going over the specs for the press launch in a month's time.

'They're well paid not to question what I do,' he muttered, making the implication clear that she had also been well paid not to question him and not to confront him.

He was damned if he'd be found wanting by someone he'd paid to be his wife…

'Are you avoiding me because of what you told me about your scar?'

The gentle enquiry—and the astuteness behind it—shocked him so much, he couldn't hide his reaction.

Her gaze darkened, piercing the protective layer he'd always kept around his emotions.

'So you remember that?' he growled.

The sick nausea in his stomach was nothing to the surge of fury making his chest hurt. This was why he had never confided in anyone. Why the hell had he confided in her? Giving her ammunition against him? It made no sense, and the compassion in her gaze shook him to his core.

She nodded, the emerald eyes sparking with a sympathy he despised.

He didn't need or want her pity. He'd made a staggering success of his life, despite his squalid and violent beginnings—maybe even because of them.

'I hope he paid for what he did,' she said, her voice breaking slightly, as if she were holding back tears.

'He had his reasons.' He had no desire to talk about the man who he had feared and loved in equal measure until he had realised Harry Wolfe had never wanted him any more than Daniel Smyth had.

Her eyes widened, the shocked distress calling to something deep inside him that he had no intention of acknowledging.

'What possible reason could he have for mutilating a child?' she whispered.

'He discovered I wasn't his son,' Jack said, his thumb stroking the ragged flesh—until he became aware of what he was doing and dropped his hand.

Instead of ending the conversation as he'd

hoped, Katie simply stepped towards him, invading the personal space he so desperately needed.

'That's not a reason, Jack,' she said softly. 'To hurt someone who loved him.'

'I didn't love him.' The denial scraped over the jagged boulder which had formed in his throat. 'He was a violent, abusive bastard to me and my mother for as long as I can remember. I was glad I wasn't his. It gave me an excuse to leave that place and never look back.'

Except he *had* looked back, many times, the brutal shame still lurking in some dark, unbidden corner of his heart. The picture he'd tried so hard to suppress flickered into his memory of his mother's face the last time he'd seen her. The once soft, beautiful skin had been strained and tear-streaked, puffy with exhaustion, desperation and the drugs she'd used to forget as the paramedics had arrived.

Don't tell them who did this, honey. Please don't, or he'll be even angrier.

Who had really been the monster? The man who had destroyed his mother, or the boy who had forced her into his arms then left to save himself?

Stepping closer still, Katherine placed her warm palm on his scarred cheek. 'I'm glad you got out.'

He jerked back, jolted out of the miserable reminiscence. Grasping her wrist, he pulled her hand from his face. 'Don't…' he said.

She stared at him, her eyes bold and unashamed.

Vicious sensation prickled across his sunwarmed shoulders and sank deep into his abdomen, the need as swift and visceral as it had ever been.

To hell with it. There was no containing it. And he'd be damned if he'd even try any longer.

'Don't touch me,' he said, his thumb pressing against the inside of her wrist, feeling the rampant pulse, her instinctive response only making the swift, visceral need all the more brutal. 'Not unless you've changed your mind about sleeping with me.'

He expected her to retreat, to fall back on the lie she'd told him before they'd arrived on the island, but instead her expression remained open and unguarded, the hunger clear and unashamed. He dragged her into his embrace, until her soft curves pressed against the hard line of his body.

She didn't flinch, didn't fight him, her breath coming in ragged pants. Then she licked her lips and the fierce arousal turned to pain, his yearning flesh hardening against her belly. He breathed in a lungful of her smell, the rich, earthy scent beneath the aroma of sun cream and sweat sending his senses into overdrive.

'Admit you want me, Katherine,' he demanded. 'And I'll stop avoiding you.'

Shocked arousal dilated the vivid green of her irises to black. 'I want you.'

His raw groan echoed across the pool terrace as he lifted her into his arms. 'Wrap your legs around my waist.'

She grasped his shoulders and obeyed him as he captured her mouth, devouring her in greedy bites—the way he'd dreamed of doing for days. He thrust his tongue deep to capture her startled sobs and marched across the pool terrace and into the house.

All that mattered now was sinking into her again, driving them both to oblivion and claiming what was his so he could forget the things she'd wrenched out of him.

She didn't know him—not really. And he didn't want her to know him.

This was all he wanted from her, the only connection that mattered to him.

This is dangerous, and you know it.

Katie's brain tried to engage, but the rush of adrenaline and the swell of tenderness was unstoppable as Jack strode into the house and took the stairs to the mezzanine.

Her heart pumped hard, sensation spreading through her body like wildfire. He held her easily, as if she weighed nothing at all, while his kisses devoured her neck, her collarbone.

At last, he dumped her onto the huge, canopied bed where she'd slept alone the night before.

A glass wall looked out onto the bay, the diamond-white sand giving way to the iridescent turquoise sea. She lay dazed and disorientated as he dragged off the towel. His arousal jutted out from his belly, thick and long and aggressive, somehow. Her gaze lifted to the tortured expression on his face that matched the giddy, relentless desperation in her heart.

Why had she insisted on provoking him, even knowing the danger? But she couldn't look away from the tight, barely leashed need on his face and the thick jut of his erection as he joined her on the bed. Pushing her legs apart with one insistent thigh, he dragged her shorts off. Then he groaned, thumbing her turgid nipples through her swimsuit.

'A one-piece?' he murmured. 'Just kill me now.'

A chuckle rose up her torso at his look of consternation, but then strangled in her throat as he lifted the swollen flesh over the top of the suit and traced his tongue around one yearning peak.

'Tell me if it hurts...' He growled as he gathered the hardening peak between his lips.

'It doesn't!' she gasped as he suckled with unbearable tenderness.

She rose off the bed as the drawing sensation arrowed into the molten spot between her thighs, the ache intensifying.

She squirmed and writhed, the pleasure too much and yet not enough as he feasted on one nipple then the other.

She grasped his head to drag him closer and dislodged the glasses.

He swore softly and levered himself off the bed. 'Wait there. And take that damn one-piece off. I need to get my lenses in,' he said. 'I'll be damned if I do this blind.'

She lay on the bed, trying to gather her wits, or what was left of them. But her panting breaths only made her feel more light-headed, more disorientated.

She should call a halt to this—forget the harsh sadness in his eyes when he had told her about his past. But something stopped her, and she knew it was a great deal more than just the promise of having the desperate hunger finally fed.

She still lay there, the emotions churning in her gut, her heart pummelling her ribs when he returned. The glasses were gone—the intimidating erection wasn't.

She drew herself into a sitting position. 'Perhaps we shouldn't...'

'I think we both know it's too late for that,' he cut her off, then grasped her wrist and dragged her off the bed until they stood toe to toe. She'd lost her sandals on the way into the house, her bare toes sinking into the deep carpet, but his urgent erection was nowhere near as overwhelming as the turmoil in his eyes.

He cupped her cheek with a shocking gentleness

that weakened her knees. He threaded his fingers into her hair and the loose knot tumbled down.

'We need this,' he said.

She opened her mouth, wanting to deny it, but then he placed his mouth on the pummelling pulse by her collarbone. The protest lodged in her throat as he dragged off her shirt... And the words that would release her from the silken web imprisoning her refused to come.

He peeled the suit from her body in one forceful glide.

In the half-light of her granny's cottage at nightfall, her body had been sheltered, obscured, but here the glaring sunlight spotlighted every flaw, every imperfection. But he didn't seem to notice, his urgent hands stroking her to fever pitch.

At last he found her sex and began to torture and torment with insistent fingers.

He sank to his knees and cupped her hips before prising her legs apart. But a position that should have made him less dominant only made him more so as his gaze locked with hers and his tongue trailed up the inside of her thigh.

She shivered, sinking her fingers into his damp hair. She shuddered as he lapped and lathed, finally parting the curls hiding her sex to lick at her clitoris at last. The swell built, staggering in its intensity, shattering the last of her resistance and charging through her body on a tidal wave of stunned pleasure.

As the brutal orgasm subsided, she stood, shaking, exhausted. He rose to his feet to tower over her. 'It's too late to escape me, Red. You're mine now, in the only way that matters.'

She should reject the brutal cynicism, the claim of ownership. She would never belong to any man—but she no longer had the strength to resist it.

Pressing her back on the bed, he climbed over her. Scooping up her legs, he lifted her knees, spreading her wide open for the brutal invasion. He anchored the huge erection deep in one slow, mind-altering thrust, impaling her to the hilt.

Her body contracted, struggling to adjust to the thick invasion, while dragging him deeper still as she clung to his broad shoulders. He began to move in a harsh, relentless rhythm, his breathing as ragged as her own.

The pleasure rose again with brutal speed, furious, overwhelming, rushing towards her on another wave. Her fingers dug into broad, sweat-slicked muscles, trying to concentrate on the physical. But the turmoil in her chest refused to subside as the tsunami bowled over her again, and she heard him shout out as he collapsed on top of her.

Katie lay dazed for what felt like an eternity, Jack's shoulder digging into her collarbone.

She drew in a shuddering breath and let it

out again, waiting as the serene wave of after-glow faded into something hollow and deeply unsettling.

Groaning, Jack pulled out of her at last. She felt the loss of connection instantly. After gathering the last remnants of her sanity around her, the flight instinct that had deserted her so comprehensively minutes ago returned in a rush. She edged to the side of the bed.

He'd torn the swimming costume when he'd dragged it off her, so she scooped up the shorts. Embarrassment heated her cheeks as she tugged them on, forced to wear them without underwear.

'Hey, where are you going?'

The gruff voice behind her had her glancing over her shoulder.

He reclined in the bed, the white sheet lying low on his hips, one arm slung behind his head, the other flat against his stomach, a watchful, questioning light in those crystal-blue eyes.

Her thighs twitched and her sex pulsed, making her aware of the soreness where he had plundered her so convincingly.

'For a walk,' she said, desperate to get away from him and the brutal feeling of connection.

He wasn't the boy who had been scarred by a violent stepfather. He was a forceful, dynamic and scarily controlled man who was going to become a father himself but had no intention of becoming part of his child's life. Perhaps his past explained why he didn't *want* to be a father, but it also meant he was less likely to change his mind.

As she went to stand, he lurched across the bed and grasped her wrist.

She lifted her hand, trying to wrestle it free of his grasp. 'Jack, I have to…'

'Don't go,' he said, the request cutting her protest off at the knees. Her hand dropped to the bed, still manacled in his. 'Stay.'

'I don't think that's a good idea,' she said, but she could hear the foolish hesitation in her own voice. What was wrong with her? What was she hoping was going to happen?

And how could the yearning still be there? Now they'd fed the hunger?

Except it didn't feel fed…not even close. Her gaze lingered on the smooth contours of his chest, the bunch of muscle and sinew, the faded ink.

'Why not?' he asked, but then his lips twitched, as if he were holding back a grin. 'We're on our honeymoon.'

'Yes, but it's not a real honeymoon,' she countered, still trying to cling to what was left of her common sense. Even as a niggling voice at the back of her head kept saying… *Why not stay and find out if there could be more?*

Hadn't they both been running for too long? Didn't she owe it to their child, his child, at least to try?

He fascinated her—his facets, his mood

swings and all the carefully guarded secrets that lurked behind his eyes. She was attracted like a moth to a flame, the danger only making him more intriguing.

He had given her something this afternoon, a small glimpse of himself. How could that be bad?

'Right now, it feels real enough,' he murmured, his voice a rough burr of sound that seemed to scrape across her skin like sandpaper.

Sitting up, he turned her body until they sat together on the side of the bed, his thighs bracketing her hips, one large hand resting on the barely-there curve of her belly, his chest hot against her back. He hooked her hair behind her ear to expose her neck and nuzzled the sensitive skin over the galloping pulse.

'Come on, Katherine. We might as well make the most of this chemistry while it lasts,' he murmured. 'What have we got to lose?'

'But what if it never ends?' she asked, then realised how gauche that sounded when he chuckled.

'You don't have a lot of sexual experience, do you, Red?'

She shifted round, trying to see his face. 'I have enough,' she said indignantly.

He skimmed his finger down her nose, the gesture gentle and mocking, but also strangely approving.

'This won't last,' he said, his eyes flaring with

fierce need. 'Nothing this good ever does.' The echo of regret made her heart pulse hard.

'But this wasn't supposed to be real,' she finally managed to blurt out as the heat gathered and twisted while his lips roamed over her skin, making her tender sex ache all over again. 'That was the deal.'

Did he know what he was asking of her? What he was risking?

His soft chuckle echoed across her nape before he bit softly into her earlobe.

'Deals can be renegotiated,' he said. 'If both parties are amenable.'

His hand drifted beneath the open fly of her shorts, his fingers delving, exploring.

She jolted as he found her clitoris, still wet, swollen and far too sensitive.

She gripped his wrist, trying to stop the devious, devastating caresses that were turning her into a mass of desperation all over again. How did he do that? So easily? How did he make her forget all her priorities, make her stop thinking and only feel?

His hand stilled, but his voice still held the hint of amusement and the purr of command as it whispered across her neck. 'Shh, Katherine. Let me prove to you how good this is.'

Her grip loosened, her head dropping against his shoulder as the last of her objections drifted away on the tide of pleasure, the pulse of emotion. He circled the slick flesh—tantalising, tormenting. Tortured sobs issued from her lips as a cloud covered the sun and she saw their reflection in the window glass.

His big body surrounded hers, his tanned hand working against the open fly of her shorts with ruthless efficiency. His mouth suckled and nipped at the pulse in her neck, but the sensation concentrated in her sex. His other hand covered one naked breast, moulding the round weight then rolling and plucking the engorged nipple, sending more darts to her core. She quivered and moaned as her back arched, pushing herself instinctively into the devastating caresses—wanting, needing, more.

'Please... I...' she whispered, begging him to take the ache away.

'That's it, Red. Come for me again,' he demanded, just as his fingers found the epicentre at her core. The ache exploded, the earthquake of pleasure too pure, too strong.

She flew again, bowing back, crying out, the climax overwhelming her. And knew, whatever came next, she couldn't run from him any more.

Later, much later—after a shared shower, an exhilarating ride out into the bay on the motor launch, a meal on the terrace delivered on mopeds by two waiters who disappeared as soon as they had served it and another tumultuous and exhausting lovemaking session—Katie lay in Jack's arms again and listened to the slow murmur of his breathing.

Somehow she'd agreed to make this a real honeymoon... Or rather, real enough.

The sun dropped towards the sea, the kaleidoscope of red and orange reflected off the dark water, but felt nowhere near as dramatic as the conflagration in her chest.

Had she done the right thing, giving in to her fascination with Jack? How could she not...? When she was so tired of fighting it? Tired of pretending the need didn't exist? And tired of denying the compassion she felt for the boy who lurked inside the man?

'Consider the terms of our contract renegotiated, Katherine,' he murmured against her nape, his hand absently caressing her stomach where their baby grew.

Her heart bumped into her throat.

But when he relaxed behind her, his breathing becoming deep and even against her back, it took her for ever to fall asleep too. Because she knew she'd just taken a step into unguarded, unknowable territory. A step into no man's land, despite all her best intentions. Just as she had done when she had left her father's house all those years ago.

On one level it terrified her. The only question now was, could she be strong enough, smart enough, patient enough, resilient enough to find out if Jack might one day take that step with her...or would it be another step she would have to take alone?

CHAPTER TWELVE

One month later

'WHERE IS MRS WOLFE?' Jack demanded of Katherine's housekeeper, Mrs Goulding, as he marched into her office in the basement. He'd searched the Mayfair house and couldn't find his wife.

'She had an appointment in Harley Street this afternoon,' Mrs Goulding replied.

The anticipation—which had been expanding under his breastbone and making it virtually impossible for him to concentrate on the endless conference calls he'd had that day to finalise the last of the Smyth-Brown takeover—popped like an overblown balloon.

'Is everything okay?' he asked, his impatience—because she hadn't been here when he had arrived, as she normally would be—turning into something else.

He'd left her in the early hours of the morning to return to his penthouse after spending most of the night ravishing her. She'd been deeply asleep, which wasn't like her at all. She'd been working hard recently on her new business after taking the decision to open a small shop in Knightsbridge to make her online bakery brand more visible.

It had been three weeks since they'd returned from their so-called honeymoon in the Maldives and the need hadn't abated one bit. If anything it had got considerably worse. But what was perhaps a great deal more concerning was the unsettled, agitated feeling that had begun to assail him whenever Katherine was out of his sight.

He had become obsessed with his trophy wife.

The rest of the week in the Maldives—after she had agreed to sleep with him—had been nothing short of idyllic. But not for the reasons he would have assumed.

She had been as eager as he to indulge their sexual connection. In fact, she had thrown herself into it with as much enthusiasm as he had. They'd made love on the beach, by the pool and on the power launch while anchored off one of the deserted islands on the atoll, after a morning spent snorkelling on the reef. And every night, every morning and many of the hours in between, when he'd woken dreaming of her, to find her body curved into his, wet and eager as he woke her.

She hadn't denied him once, had even initiated the contact on more than one occasion, her tentative, adorably artless attitude to sex becoming almost as demanding and adventurous as his by the time the trip had ended.

He'd remained living in the penthouse—to get the distance he needed—and she hadn't objected. He'd almost been disappointed when she had failed even to comment on his decision. While he still had his clothes in the penthouse, and despite his best intentions to ensure he continued to live his own life, he spent every night with her in Grosvenor Square before returning home, often in the early hours of the morning, to wash and change before heading to his office.

Keeping his belongings in the penthouse had become inconvenient, so he'd been forced to move some items into the house here. Again, she hadn't commented, hadn't pushed. She probed occasionally about his past, his childhood, but had allowed him to deflect those questions easily. And, when she had made offhand comments about the baby, the pregnancy, she hadn't pressed when he had failed to engage.

He should have felt fine. Their life was just as he wanted it, just as he had envisaged it when proposing this marriage.

So why wasn't he content?

Perhaps because it wasn't just the sex that had captivated him since they had returned. He also enjoyed the conversations in the evenings when he arrived from the office to find her in her study, video calling her team or strategising with her marketing manager, or in the kitchen, rustling up something delicious after giving the chef a night off.

During those conversations he had discovered exactly how smart, erudite and witty Katherine was, her intelligence and single-mindedness a match for his own. They'd argued about politics, culture and sport, and had talked at length about her business plans and her long-term goals. She'd come to him with queries, questions, hiring problems and strategy suggestions, and he'd been happy to help.

And she'd quizzed him about his own business. Because he had deflected any personal questions about his childhood, he had refrained from asking about hers, even though he was hopelessly curious now about *her* past. He wanted to know how she had survived after being kicked out of her home at seventeen. And how she had managed to retain such an optimistic and surprisingly naive attitude towards the generosity of the human spirit when he most certainly had not.

And why couldn't he stop thinking about her even now?

It would be pathetic, if it weren't so disturbing.

'I don't believe anything is wrong, sir,' the

housekeeper said. 'It may be a scheduled appointment.'

It may be? What if it wasn't? Surely she would have told him if it was routine? She'd mentioned her antenatal appointments in the past. And he'd made a point of not engaging with the information. He didn't want to give her false hopes where his involvement with the child was concerned. But, even so, he knew she would have said something if she was going to be late home. They had a ball to attend tonight, which was why he had arrived home early... That and the fact he seemed less and less able to stay at the office when he knew she awaited him at the house.

Katherine had been tired last night, after returning from a concert they'd attended at the O2. He'd sourced the box seats because he'd caught her dancing to one of the famous band's songs a few weeks ago, and had watched her unobserved, charmed by the sight. He should have left her alone last night and returned to the penthouse after dropping her off, but he hadn't been able to stop himself, the excuse of ensuring she was okay having morphed into something urgent and unstoppable once they'd got to her bedroom.

The guilt that had been sitting at the back of his mind all day tightened its claws around his neck now like a malevolent beast.

Her subdued mood last night had left him holding her a little tighter as he waited for her to drift to sleep in the early hours of the morning. And it had been harder than ever to pull himself out of the bed and leave her to return to his own place.

Deepening their relationship was not part of the deal. And not something he wanted. Because it would only complicate things when he had to let her go. But perhaps he should have stayed with her last night.

'How was she this morning?' he barked, not quite able to keep the frantic urgency out of his voice.

Damn. If he'd woken up with her he would know the answer to this question. Why hadn't he stayed?

'She seemed tired, Mr Wolfe,' the house-keeper said. 'But then she had an early morning meeting, so she had to leave an hour ahead of her usual schedule.'

'She... What time did she get up?' he rasped, the malevolent beast beating on his ribs now.

'Six o'clock.'

He swore under his breath, the guilt and panic turning to anger. She hadn't fallen asleep until two a.m. Why hadn't she told him she had to be up so early? He wouldn't have kept her up half the night if she had.

'Is there a problem, Mr Wolfe?' the house-keeper asked.

Yes, there's a damn problem. My wife may be seriously unwell and it's my fault. And her fault, for not telling me to leave her alone.

His mind reeled, the unguarded feelings starting to overwhelm him.

'No,' he snapped. He headed back through the house towards the entrance hall, tugging his phone out of his pocket en route and speed-dialling Katherine's number. But as he charged down the hallway, intending to drive straight to Harley Street, an echo of his phone's ring tone sounded.

He stopped in the entrance hall to see his wife standing by the front door.

'Katherine!' He charged towards her and grasped her shoulders as the panic surged. 'Are you okay? What were you doing at the doctor's?'

'Jack?' Her eyebrows launched up her forehead, but he could see the fatigue still shadowing her eyes. 'What are you doing here so early?' she said, apropos to absolutely nothing.

'I asked first,' he said. 'What's wrong?' He forced himself to stare at the slight mound of her stomach, which he had noticed more and more in the last few weeks whenever they made love. 'Is it the pregnancy?'

'Nothing's wrong,' she said, but he could hear

the weary note in her voice as she tried to shrug off his hold. His grip tightened.

'Jack, you need to let me go,' she said with strained patience, as if he were holding her for the fun of it. As if his head wasn't starting to explode. Why the hell couldn't she give him a straight answer? Was something seriously wrong and she didn't want to tell him?

'My phone's ringing and I need to answer it,' she added, cutting through the flash flood of disaster scenarios in his head.

He cursed, letting go of her with one hand, to fish his own phone out of his pocket and turn it off.

The confusion in her eyes darkened. 'Why were you calling me?'

'Why the hell do you think?' he shouted, frustration and fury pushing up his throat to party with the guilt and panic. 'You're always at home when I get here in the evening. You weren't here, and then Mrs Goulding told me you were at the doctor's and I—'

'It was a routine scan,' she interrupted.

The panic babbling stopped so abruptly, his fingers loosened.

She shrugged out of his hold.

His temper ignited. 'Well, that's just great!' he said, pushing the guilt back down his throat with an effort. 'Why didn't you tell me you had an appointment?' Had she planned to freak him out deliberately?

Was this some kind of dumb test? To push him into admitting she meant something to him? Something more than they'd originally agreed on?

Because of course she did. Maybe this arrangement had no future, but he'd been sleeping with her every night for over a month—hell, he'd even started to neglect his business so he could spend more time with her.

The endless meetings and problems he had to attend to, being available twenty-four-seven to his managers and advisors, had become a chore over the last three weeks. He had turned down a ton of business trips—had even chosen not to travel to the product launch in Tokyo of a new tech company he'd acquired last year when it had clashed with the opening of Katherine's shop. Because he hadn't been able to bear to spend forty-eight hours away from her.

Of course, he could have insisted as per their original contract, that she travel with him. But he simply hadn't had the heart to tear her away from her business when she was clearly so excited about developing it.

And then there were their weekends, when he'd started to make excuses to be with her. He'd always worked at weekends in the past. But gradually, after they'd returned from the Maldives, he'd begun concocting reasons to contact her, spend quality time with her. And not just to coax her into bed. They had taken drives in the countryside, long walks in the park, watched movies in the house's basement cinema, or frolicked in the lap pool he'd had installed in the two-hundred-foot garden.

Yet another sign of how dependent on her company he had become.

He'd tried to convince himself it was still all about the sex—the quality time just an intriguing prelude to jumping each other. But this incessant need that never seemed to end—no matter how many times he took her, how many times they took each other—had forced him to realise that wasn't the whole truth. She meant something to him. Much more than she should. But instead of looking guilty or even contrite, she stared back at him now as if he'd lost the plot.

'Why would I tell you about the scan, Jack?' she asked with a weary resignation that made his ribs contract around his thundering heart. 'When you're not interested.'

She went to pass him, but he grabbed her arm. 'Wait a minute. What is that supposed to mean?'

'Why don't you figure it out?' she said, the sudden snap in her tone surprising him. He shook off the residual hum of guilt. *He* wasn't the one in the wrong here. She should have told him she had a doctor's appointment. So he hadn't had to find out from the housekeeper. End of.

'You think I don't care about your welfare?' he demanded, the turmoil of emotions making his anger surge. 'Of course I care. I care about you. A lot. *There*. Are you happy?'

But, instead of looking smug, her chin tucked into her chest as she sighed.

When her gaze lifted back to his, he could see the shocking sheen of tears. The sight punctured the self-righteous fury with the precision of a high velocity bullet, leaving shock in its wake.

'No, Jack,' she said, so quietly he almost couldn't hear her. 'I'm not happy.'

A single tear slipped from the corner of her eye before she could wipe it away with an impatient fist. And the shock reverberated in his chest like an earthquake.

She dug her teeth into her bottom lip to stop it trembling, her gaze bold and determined, but also somehow broken. The emerald-green, sparkling with all the tears she refused to shed, only crucified him more.

This was what he'd been determined to guard against—why he'd snuck out of her bed each night even though the desire to hold her, to keep her safe, had been all but overwhelming. Why he'd forced himself not to ask all the questions he wanted answers to about her father, her past, about the strong, clever teenager he wished he'd known back when they'd both been still too young to protect themselves.

And, because of that, he heard himself ask a question he knew he shouldn't want the answer to…but did.

'Why aren't you happy?'

Katie stared at her husband, her limbs saturated with exhaustion. The sight of him—strong and indomitable and hopelessly wary—was making sensation flutter and glow in her belly even now.

He'd taken off his jacket and tie, his short hair stuck up in spikes as if he'd run his fingers through it several times. His gaze roamed over her, his eyes searching and a little wild, as he pressed a warm hand to her shoulder then stroked his thumb down her arm.

The prickle of sensation which was always there when he touched her rolled through her. But with it came the fierce pulse of emotion she no longer had any control over.

She'd thrown herself into this relationship in the weeks since they had returned from the Maldives, forced the emotion down and let the heat take over so she could give them both time. To get to know each other, to feel comfortable. But as they'd begun to settle into a routine, the more Jack had let her see of that runaway boy who needed love the way she had, the harder it had been not to push, not to probe, not to beg for more.

Every time he made love to her with such fervour then left her sleeping alone. Every time they had a discussion about business, marketing or her latest cupcake recipe but he'd deflected any questions he deemed too personal. Every time she sent him an email with her latest schedule of antenatal appointments and scans but she got no response.

She blinked, the prickle of sensation turning to something deep, fluid and even more disturbing.

She didn't *want* to feel this way. Didn't want him to show her this side of himself. A caring, tender, nurturing side she was sure he didn't even realise he possessed. Because the more she saw of it, the more real their relationship seemed.

Like the time he'd caught her dancing in the kitchen and she'd seen the spontaneous, boyish smile curving his lips. Or the times he had suggested, more and more of late, that they do something together at the weekend, that he didn't need to work. Like the tension in his jaw she'd begun to notice whenever she yawned and he asked if she were okay. Or the leap of hunger and something more—something rich with relief and even joy—that turned his blue eyes to a rich cobalt when he came here each evening and found her.

And the moment last night, when she'd discovered he had paid a small fortune for tickets to a sold-out concert because he believed she liked the band that was playing. She hadn't even realised it was the same band who had done the song she had been dancing to several weeks before until he'd mentioned it oh, so casually. A part of her had been overjoyed. But another part of her had been devastated. How could he be so observant, so thoughtful, and yet not know how much it meant to her?

And how was she supposed to stop herself from falling hopelessly in love with that man?

But this afternoon had been the wake-up call she needed. The signal she had to start demanding more of him, or she would be lost. She'd seen her baby's three-dimensional image on the ultrasound equipment. She'd devoured the incredible sight of its tiny nose and mouth, the closed eyelids, its long limbs—just like its father's. She'd laughed at Dr Patel pointing out it was sucking its thumb, and shed a few stunned tears when she'd made the decision to find out the baby's sex after the doctor had told her she had a clear image of its sexual organs.

All those emotions had bombarded her—excitement, awe, wonder... And yet at the same time her heart had felt as if it were being ripped away from her chest wall. Because she'd experienced all those incredible, life-altering moments alone. Because Jack had chosen not to be there with her.

It hurt even more to see the stunned compassion on his face now, the wary confusion at her tears. And the defensiveness in his eyes. Because a part of her knew the words he had just flung at her like missiles, words which had stunned her, were true. He *did* care about her. Probably much more than he wanted to. But how could that be enough? For her or their baby?

'Why aren't you happy?' he'd asked her, as if he really didn't know.

Maybe he didn't.

She sucked in an unsteady breath, determined not to let another tear fall. She hated tears. They didn't solve anything. And she refused to be that woman who broke down rather than ask for what she wanted.

She'd been trying to have this conversation for weeks, and it had been like thumping her head against a brick wall, but he had given her an opening this time, and she would be a fool not to take it.

'You know, I saw our baby properly for the first time today on the ultrasound,' she said as conversationally as she could manage.

Something flickered in his eyes, something wary, tense and instantly guarded. But when he didn't say anything, didn't stop her or try to deflect the conversation as he always had before, the fragile bubble of hope expanded in her chest.

'Dr Patel told me what she thinks the sex is. Would you like to know?'

He stared at her, his expression unreadable.

'Of course, it's not one hundred percent, but Dr Patel was pretty sure. She said about eighty-five percent sure.' She was babbling now, but when his gaze shifted to her stomach, as she had seen it do so many times in the last few weeks as her bump had become more pronounced, the bubble grew. 'Aren't you even a little bit curious?' she asked.

His gaze lifted back to her face. He wanted to say no. She could see it in his eyes. So she blurted it out before he could stop her... 'It's a boy.'

His brows rose, the slash of colour on his cheeks hard to interpret. Was he pleased, surprised, indifferent? Why couldn't she tell even now? How did he manage to keep so much of himself back? Not just from her, but from their child? Would it always be like this?

Was this still all about that young boy he wouldn't talk about? The lost, brutalised child he'd given her a glimpse of in the Maldives and then refused to acknowledge ever since?

He looked away from her and she could see he

was struggling from the tell-tale muscle twitching in his jaw. But what was he struggling with?

'I was thinking of the name Daniel,' she ventured.

His head swung back round. 'No. I don't like that name.'

'Oh, okay,' she managed, but her heart soared. It was the most he had ever given her. The first sign he cared enough about this baby to have a preference. Maybe this didn't have to be a lost cause. Had she given up far too soon? Allowed her own feelings for him to colour the progress they'd made? Feelings that perhaps weren't as unrequited as she'd assumed. Perhaps this wasn't so much about him but about her, and her own desire to protect herself. She was letting everything get mixed up in her head because she was scared too. Scared he would reject her the way her father had. But he'd already given her so much more, without even realising it.

'If you've got any suggestions, I'm all ears,' she managed, her throat thickening with emotion again. Did he know how significant this moment was?

The discomfort in his face was clear. Obviously, he did. But then he murmured, 'I'll think about it.' He glanced at his watch. 'We're supposed to be going to the Collington Charity Ball tonight.' His penetrating gaze searched her face, the wariness returning full force. 'You're tired. If you'd rather avoid it, I can make your excuses.'

Not on your life.

Her heart galloped into her throat, the stupid bubble of hope expanding so fast it was almost choking her. He'd said he cared about her. He'd clearly freaked out when he'd thought she was ill. And he had offered an opinion about the baby's name. And okay, it *had* been reluctantly, but after weeks of what had felt like no progress she was not about to let this shining, shimmering gift horse out of her sight.

'Give me an hour to dress,' she said, and left him standing in the hallway, the weary resignation lifting off her shoulders as she all but skipped up the stairs.

It wasn't enough, but it was enough for now. This didn't have to be about his past or hers. This could be about their future. A future she suddenly felt sure was so much brighter now than it had been an hour ago in the ultrasound suite.

Jack Wolfe *could* be a father. All she had to do was let go of her own insecurities long enough to show him.

A boy?

The information reverberated in Jack's skull, doing nothing to deaden the fear that had been tormenting him for close to an hour as he paused in the doorway of his wife's suite.

She stood in the next room, checking out the

fit of her dress for tonight's ball in the mirror, unaware of his presence.

His breath got trapped in his lungs.

The rich, red satin hugged her bold curves, lifting her full breasts, accentuating her lush bottom. The pale skin revealed by the gown's plunging back and the sprinkle of freckles across her bare shoulder blades were given a pearly glow by the room's diffused lighting. He wanted to put his lips at the base of her spine, trail kisses up the delicious line of her backbone to her nape.

He knew exactly how she tasted there, in the hollow beneath her earlobe. And how she would respond—first with surprise, then with excitement, exhilaration and a hunger which matched his own—holding nothing back.

He shoved his hands into his pockets and forced himself not to walk into the room and begin unravelling her outfit. Because in the last hour the flicker of joy, of belonging, of protectiveness which always assailed him when he returned to the house in Mayfair, seemed somehow threatening in a way it never had before.

She moved, revealing the compact curve of her belly, and the fear dropped into his belly like an unexploded bomb. The jumble of emotions which had been festering for an hour collided as he recalled the hope in her eyes. The last thing he wanted to do right now was escort her to the VIP charity event, to parade her in front of a load of other men like a trophy, an acquisition, even though that was exactly what she was supposed to be.

This arrangement had always had a sell-by date. How had he lost sight of that in the last month? After tonight he would have to re-establish the emotional distance he'd lost, or how else would he be able to control the deep pulse of regret, of longing, of loneliness which was already building when he was forced to let her go?

He cleared his throat and she swung round. The brief flicker of joy in her emerald eyes that he'd seen so many times in the past few weeks wrapped around his heart, scaring him even more.

'Jack?' she whispered, the sound raw. 'Is it time to go?'

He made himself walk into the room, aware of her appreciative gaze gliding over his figure in the tailored tuxedo. 'Yes, we should probably make a move,' he said, trying to keep his tone impersonal, to cover the emotions churning inside him and stop himself from blurting out what he wanted to say to her.

This isn't a marriage of convenience any more.

But even the thought of saying those words made him feel weak and pathetic and needy.

He placed a hand on her bare shoulder, felt

her shudder of response. But, instead of placing his lips on the fluttering pulse in her collarbone, he slid his palm down her arm then lifted her fingers to his lips.

'You look beautiful,' he said as he kissed her knuckles and watched the leap of joy flicker again in her eyes at the inadequate complement.

He straightened and let her hand drop, the fear gripping his throat again.

'Jack, is something wrong?' she asked, pressing her palms against the smooth satin of the dress, her gaze far too astute.

'We need to go or we'll be late,' he said.

Her throat contracted as she swallowed. 'Okay.'

He didn't want to hurt her, but he knew he would, because he could never be the man she needed.

CHAPTER THIRTEEN

'How about Sebastian? Or Luca? I've always liked Luca,' Katie offered, excited as the chauffeur-driven car stopped in front of the ornate redbrick façade of the Drapers' Hall where the charity ball they were attending was being held.

Jack sent her a quelling look. 'We're here.'

She grinned back at him, refusing to be put off by his usual reserve when it came to talking about the baby. Talking about their son. The giddy hope had her beaming smiles and even waving at the barrage of press photographers as Jack escorted her into the hall. The smile didn't even dim as Jack led her into an imposing marble-columned ballroom, the gold leaf glimmering in the light of the chandeliers.

For once she didn't feel like a complete fraud as Jack introduced her to the array of VIP guests and business people who always gravitated towards her husband when they arrived at these sorts of events.

My husband.

Funny that tonight she actually felt like Jack's wife. And the mother of his child. Obviously this was still an arrangement, a bargain, a marriage with a sell-by date stamped on it. But they'd taken a huge step forward tonight. Not just when Jack had told her he cared about her, but when he had kissed her hand with such tenderness, such reverence, in her dressing room. She felt closer to him now than she ever had before.

She cupped her belly absently, excited about the pregnancy in a way she had never been before. What if they could do this together? What if she didn't have to do this alone?

She felt as if she were floating—with only Jack's stalwart presence by her side to anchor her to earth—as the evening sped past. She chatted enthusiastically about everything from how to bake the perfect brownie, with the French ambassador, to the wonder of Wolfe Maldives with an award-winning actress who was heading to the resort next month after her current film finished shooting. For once the small talk wasn't a chore and she didn't feel as if she was lying when she talked about her honeymoon or her husband.

But, after two hours on her feet, Katie began to flag.

'You look tired. Would you like to return home?' Jack asked but, just as she placed her fingers on his forearm for some much-needed support, about to give him a resounding yes, his muscles became rigid. His face hardened as his gaze locked on something over her shoulder.

She turned to see a tall, elegant, older man walking through the crowd straight towards them.

'Who's that?' she asked, concerned at the cold light that had entered Jack's eyes.

'No one,' he said, the bite in his tone chilling.

But, before she could say more, the man reached them. 'Mr Wolfe, I presume,' he said, the quirk of his lips doing nothing to dispel the hostile tone.

The man had a patrician handsomeness, the few lines on his tanned face making it hard to tell how old he was—probably in his mid-sixties, with his carefully styled hair more salt than pepper. There was something, though—about the line of his jaw, the powerful way he moved, the brilliant blue of his eyes—which looked familiar.

Who was he? Katie was sure she had never met him, but she instinctively didn't like him, any more than her husband seemed to.

'I understand you are now our majority share-holder…' The man paused dramatically, the cold gleam in his eyes becoming laser-sharp, then murmured, 'Son.'

Jack jolted as if he'd been shot.

'I see you thought I didn't know,' the man continued, when Jack remained silent, the enmity thick in the air. Katie's skin chilled and her stomach jumped as realisation dawned—the physical similarities between them glaringly obvious now.

Was this man Jack's biological father?

The thought stunned her on one level, but horrified her on another, because there was no joy in the meeting—on either side.

The man gave a grim chuckle, both superior and condescending. 'My dear boy, did you really believe I would allow an upstart like you to own Smyth-Brown if I didn't want you to?'

Katie hated him, whoever he was, for treating Jack with such obvious contempt. She could feel the muscles in Jack's forearm flexing beneath her fingertips as he struggled to control his reaction.

'It won't make a difference,' Jack said, the words ground out on a husk of breath. 'I intend to destroy your legacy,' he added. 'For what you did to my mother.'

Katie's heart broke at the pain she could hear in Jack's voice, and the bone-deep regret she could see etched in the rigid line of his jaw.

But, instead of being cowed by the threat, the man—Jack's father—simply smiled, the tight line of his lips devoid of humour. 'Hmm, I see. Interesting you would blame me for her idiotic decision to marry that oaf,' he said as if he were having a conversation about the weather rather than an event that had robbed Jack of his childhood. 'Although it is a pity the brute maimed you.'

'You son of a...' Jack launched forward, his anger exploding as he grabbed the older man by his lapels.

Katie grasped his arm. 'Jack, don't. He's not worth it,' she pleaded, suddenly desperate to get him away from here. To protect him from the prying eyes of the growing crowd, riveted to the developing altercation.

She knew how much Jack valued his emotional control and his standing in the business community. Something he'd worked his whole life to gain. And she suspected a public fight was just what this bastard wanted—to expose Jack as a brute, an oaf, like the man who had scarred him.

What gave him the right to do that? When he had no part in Jack's life—or the phenomenal success he had made of it?

Jack's gaze met hers and she saw the flicker of confusion beneath the fury before the anger was downgraded enough for him to release his captive so abruptly, the man stumbled backwards.

'We should leave,' Katie said gently, touching his cheek, forcing him to look at her. Her heart yearned to tell him the words she realised she should have told him weeks ago. But she couldn't say them here, so she tried to convey them telepathically.

I love you. You matter to me. Whatever he did to you doesn't. Not any more.

He nodded, but as he gripped her hand, intending to lead them both out of the ballroom, the bastard stepped into her path.

'So this is the delightful Mrs Wolfe,' the man

said, offering her his hand as if he hadn't just tried to emotionally destroy her husband. Katie ignored it.

'Daniel Smyth at your service, my dear,' he added.

Daniel.

Before she had a chance to register the name and what it might mean, his cold gaze skimmed over her belly then lifted back to her face, the satisfied smile even more chilling. 'Did you know, my dear, I required my son marry as part of the deal for him to acquire Smyth-Brown. I needed an heir, but I really didn't think he would be quite so accommodating as to provide me with two heirs for the price of one so soon.'

What?

'Get out of our way,' Jack snarled, shoving Smyth back as he strode past him and led her out of the ballroom, the click of camera phones and the man's cruel laughter following in their wake.

'Do you really believe you can destroy my legacy, boy?' he shouted after them, sounding vaguely mad. 'When you *are* my legacy?'

Katie felt stunned, shaky, disorientated, her mind a mass of confusing emotions as Jack led her to the waiting car and helped her inside.

'Jack… Why—?' she began as the car pulled away from the kerb, suddenly desperate to contain the fear contracting around her ribs and making it hard to breathe.

'I don't want to talk about it,' he cut her off, the tone rigid with barely leashed fury as the car drove down Piccadilly towards home.

Except it isn't his home.

Her body trembled as her hands strayed to her belly.

It's my home and our baby's home. Not his. Because he doesn't want it to be. Any more than he will ever want us.

Her mind struggled to engage with the thoughts careering around in her head. The emotions battered her as the hope she'd nurtured so diligently and so pointlessly for so long finally began to die.

He sat beside her saying nothing, offering no explanation, no solace, no comfort.

The hideous things that had happened to him as a child didn't give her a connection with him, she realised. They didn't have a shared pain after both having been rejected by their fathers. This was *his* pain. A pain he guarded so jealously, so relentlessly, he had married her just to destroy the man who had caused it.

The silence stretched, creating a chasm between them, until the distance felt like millions of miles instead of only a few feet.

The car pulled into the driveway of the Grosvenor Square house. Jack got out, dismissed the chauffeur and walked round the car to open her door.

She stepped out into the night, still dazed. His

warm palm settled on her back to direct her into the house, the traitorous ripple only damning her more as he closed the front door and helped her off with her wrap.

'Thank God that's over with,' he said, his hands cupping her stomach as he dragged her back against his body, his lips finding the rampant pulse in her neck.

She jolted as ripples flooded her core at the feel of his already burgeoning erection pressing into her back.

His mouth devoured the spot under her earlobe he knew was supremely sensitive.

'Let's go to bed,' he suggested, but the raw, seductive command—one she had succumbed to so many times before—finally tore away the last of the fog until all that was left was the pain.

And the stark, gruelling light of truth.

'No,' she said, lurching out of his arms, wrenching herself away from the traitorous need.

'Damn it. I need you tonight, Katherine,' he said, his voice raw, his expression more transparent than she had ever seen it before.

She could see the hurt, the anger, the bitter confusion and the desperation the encounter with his father had caused. But she could also see in the rigid line of his jaw, in the anger sparking in his eyes, that this wasn't about her, about them, and it never had been.

She was nothing more than a temporary port

in a storm, their marriage nothing more than a convenient means for him to get his revenge for everything he'd suffered in childhood. Her heart broke for that brutalised child…but there was another child now, one who needed her love and support more.

She steeled herself against the desire to soothe, to console, to take the pain away the only way he would let her. And forced herself to say what she had to say.

'I can't do this any more, Jack. You need to leave.'

'What…? Why?' Jack yelled, the stubborn refusal on Katherine's face—and the pulse of desperation swelling in his groin—all but crucifying him.

'Because it's not me you need, Jack,' she said, her voice breaking on the words and only crucifying him more. 'It's your revenge.'

The fury surged. The fury that had been building ever since Daniel Smyth had strolled towards him with that smug, entitled smile on his face and Jack had been forced to face the sickening realisation that the son of a bitch had played him all along.

He knew who I was. Right from the start.

Daniel Smyth had got the board to insist Jack marry above his station so he could make the kid from a run-down council estate whom he had discarded before he'd even been born somehow wor-

thy to become his heir. And Jack had eventually
fallen right into the trap.

But that horrifying revelation, the cruel trick
he'd allowed himself to fall for, wasn't nearly as
gutting as the closed expression on Katherine's
face now.

If only he could just lose himself in her. Forget about tonight, about his past, about the whole
sick, stupid mess. He knew none of it would matter any more. After all, he hadn't really married
her to get the shares. He'd married her for a host
of other reasons. But as he lifted his hand to touch
her cheek, to draw her back in, she stepped back.

'When you said you didn't like the name Daniel, I thought we were having a discussion about
our son.'

He let his hand drop. So they were back to that.
Katherine, I told you I can't—'

'But tonight I found out,' she cut him off, the
quiver of regret in her hushed tone crushing him,
I found out it had nothing to do with him. It was
just another part of your past you won't allow me
to see.'

'I told you on our wedding night what I can
offer the child,' he said, even though it felt like a
lie now. 'And what I can't.'

She simply stared at him, the gleam of tears
almost more than he could bear. 'I know,' she
said, so softly he almost didn't hear her. 'And I

believed you then. But that was before I fell in love with you.'

'You…' The flood of need hit him square in the chest. But right behind it was the fear. 'No, you don't…' he said, locking away all the emotions he couldn't afford to feel.

One side of her mouth quirked in a sad half-smile, but the sense of hopelessness hovered like a dark cloud in the hallway. 'I spent the whole of my childhood trying to make my father love me. I can't do that with you, Jack. I won't.' Her hand covered her stomach where their child grew. 'I have to protect myself and my child. I don't want you here any more.'

She turned and walked away from him.

He stood, rigid with shock and anger for several seconds, desperate to chase after her, to make her want him, the way he had so many times before.

But the scar burned on his cheek, the agony real again, and so raw.

He'd begged Harry Wolfe to want him, to care about him, because he'd felt so scared. So desperate. And all it had done was left him more alone. He'd be damned if he'd make that mistake a second time.

She would come back to him. On his terms. And, until she did, he would survive without her.

But as he marched out of the house, and

slammed the door behind him, it felt as if part of his heart was being wrenched from his body.

The bitter irony was, it was the part of his heart he thought he had killed a long time ago.

CHAPTER FOURTEEN

'GORINDA, I NEED you to speak to Dr Patel's office again. I'm paying the damn bills for my wife's care. I expect to be given regular updates on her condition and I've heard nothing in two weeks,' Jack announced as he marched past his PA into his office.

Two damned weeks Katherine had been sulking. And he was through playing nice, with her or the obstetrician who was charging a fortune for her care. He needed to know she was okay, that was all. Was it too much to ask he be kept informed?

'Mr Wolfe, I've spoken to Dr Patel's administrator several times already.' Jack glanced up from his desk to see his PA's harassed expression. 'I'm afraid she says they can't give you updates on Mrs Wolfe's care without your wife's permission. It's a matter of patient confidentiality.'

'She specifically asked I not be informed?' Jack demanded, the shock combining with the frustration and fury...

The last two weeks had seemed like two years. He'd waited for her to contact him, to call him, to ask him to return to the house in Mayfair.

But she hadn't.

He wasn't sleeping, was barely eating, the yearning to hold her, to make love to her, even to see the changes the pregnancy had made to her body, so intense he could barely function.

For two weeks he'd waited for the yearning to stop so he could return to who he had been before he had met her.

A man alone. A man apart.

But, as he stared at his PA's flushed face, the brutal stab of rejection made him realise that Katherine had destroyed that man—somehow—so comprehensively, he didn't feel like a success any more. He didn't even feel happy in his own skin.

The unfulfilled desire, the physical longing that woke him from fitful dreams—leaving him hard, ready, aching and groping for her in his bed, only to find it empty—was bad enough. But the emotions he couldn't control, the nightmares he couldn't contain, were so much worse. The thought of a lifetime without her smile, her quick wit, her passion, or her companionship, was destroying him from within. And he didn't know how to overcome it. Hell, he even missed her smart mouth and her absolute refusal to do as she was told.

'Apparently she did, Mr Wolfe,' Gorinda replied, sounding almost as weary as he felt.

So Katherine had cut him loose. She'd told him she loved him. But she'd lied.

Devastation hit him.

He thrust his fingers through his hair, only to become aware his hands were shaking. How had she come to mean so much to him when she was never meant to? And how did he make this pain stop now?

He got up from his desk to stare out at the City's skyline—the gothic splendour of Tower Bridge, the gleaming mirrored sheen of The Shard on the opposite bank. It was a view that had once had the power to excite and motivate him, to make him proud of how far he'd come, but today, like every day for the last fortnight, the view seemed dull and listless, ostentatious and unimpressive.

'Dr Patel's receptionist did mention Mrs Wolfe is going to be at the clinic this morning,' Gorinda added. 'Perhaps you could join her there? To find out how she is?'

He swung round at the tentative suggestion to find Gorinda watching him with sympathy in her warm brown eyes.

But I don't want to be a part of the baby's life...

The automatic thought echoed in his head. But even thinking it felt like a lie now. It wasn't that he didn't want to be a part of this baby's life, it was that he was scared to be. Sure he'd fail at fatherhood… The way he'd failed at so much else.

'Okay,' he heard himself say.

And suddenly it all seemed so simple.

He *had* to fix this. To hell with his pride, his fear of fatherhood, his fear of asking her—no, *begging* her—to take him back, his fear of letting her see the frightened boy instead of the man he had become… None of it meant anything any more without her.

Why had it taken him so long to realise she had always been what was missing in his life?

'Rearrange my schedule and text me the address,' he said as he charged back out of the office. Of course, he had absolutely no idea *how* he was going to fix it. Or even if he could fix it. He'd just have to wing it, he thought, with a great deal more confidence than he felt.

'Yes, sir,' Gorinda replied.

If Katherine didn't want to see him, he'd just have to deal with that when he got to the clinic. But he couldn't stay away from her… Or the baby… Not a moment longer…

'I'm sorry, Mr Wolfe, your wife is having a private consultation.'

'I don't care.'

Katie shifted on the bed at the shouted comments coming from outside the ultrasound suite.

'What on earth...?' Dr Patel murmured as she put down the tube of gel she had been about to put on Katie's stomach and clicked off the machine.

But before either she or Katie could do anything more the door burst open and Jack strode in.

'Mr Wolfe! I'm sorry, you'll have to leave...' The doctor began, but Jack marched right past her, sat down in the chair beside the bed and lifted Katie's hand.

'Let me stay, Katherine. I want to meet our son,' he said, his voice thick with desperation, his eyes wild with urgency and something else... something so naked and unguarded, she wondered for a moment if she was dreaming. If she had conjured up this moment from weeks of crying herself to sleep each night.

'Jack...' she finally rasped.

'Please,' he said, and the gentle buzz of his kiss jolted her out of her trance.

'Could you leave us for a minute?' she said to Dr Patel, somehow managing to remain calm while she struggled to sit up and place a sheet over her belly.

Dr Patel nodded and left the room.

'Jack, what are you doing here?' she managed around the painful lump in her throat.

He looked distraught, she realised. But beneath the wild intensity in his expression she could also see determination. And need.

He placed his palm on her belly and rubbed the sheet so gently, she felt tears sting her eyes. 'I want to meet him too,' he said. 'Please, let me.'

She placed her hand over his, but as the joy throbbed heavily in her chest right behind it was the brutal weight of sadness, the hollow ache she had struggled to come to terms with for so long.

'Okay,' she said.

She wanted Jack to be part of his baby's life. And whatever had made him change his mind, she would always be grateful for it. But she knew there was so much else she wanted from him that she could never have. And she couldn't let the hope back in again, or it would destroy her.

'Thank you,' he said, his head dropping down until his forehead rested on her belly. He caressed the bump, his shoulders shuddering with the release of emotion. 'I'm so sorry for being such a coward.'

'Jack, it's okay.' She touched a shaky hand to his head and let her fingers stroke the short silky strands, her heart shattering in her chest. 'I would never stop you from being a part of the baby's life. You can come with me to the scans from now on. And once the baby's born you can have all the visitation rights you want.'

He lifted his head suddenly, dislodging her hand. 'But I don't want visitation rights,' he said.

'Why not?' she asked, her throat so clogged with emotion now, she could barely talk.

He whisked away the tear that had fallen from her lid. 'Because I want us to be a family. I want to move in with you, have a real marriage, stop running and start building something that will last.'

'Really?' she said but, even as the balloon of hope expanded so much that it began to hurt, the insecurities she thought she'd jettisoned so long ago flooded back.

'Of course, Katherine,' he said, as if the answer she had failed to grasp was obvious. His face softened. 'I've been an idiot. Too much of a coward, to tell you the truth. That I was terrified of becoming a father. Because I didn't know how…'

'Having met your biological father,' Katherine said, the anger that still lingered after their encounter with Daniel Smyth sharpening her words, 'I understand why you might be wary. But you're not like him, Jack. You never could be.'

'I know,' he said. 'Which is why I told my broker to sell the damn shares on the way here.

I don't want any part of his company. Not even to tear it to pieces.'

'You…you don't? But why?'

'Because you were right,' he said, his eyes shining. 'I don't need my revenge if I can have you instead.' His hand caressed the mound of her belly. 'And this fella too.'

His eyes met hers and she could see every single thing he was thinking for the first time ever… She saw sincerity, desire, fierce determination, even fear, but most of all desperate, unguarded hope.

'I need you, Katherine,' he said. He thrust his fingers through his hair, looking momentarily dumbfounded. 'Hell, I think I started to fall for you that first night when you were wearing that ridiculous outfit and I couldn't even see you properly. But I could sense your bravery and your boldness and I knew I wanted you, more than anything in the world.' He groaned.

'You…you do?' she croaked, so shocked by the heartfelt declaration, she could barely breathe, let alone think. But the insecurities were still there, asking… How could she trust him? How could she be enough, when she never had been for anyone before now?

'Yeah,' he said. His hand, trembling with emotion, gripped hers so tightly, it was as if he was holding her heart. 'I do.'

She shook her head but, despite the love that

flooded through her, she tugged her fingers out of his. 'How can you be sure?'

'What? What do you mean?' he asked, his voice raw.

'How do you know I'm enough now, when I wasn't before?'

'Stop it, Katherine,' he said, looking desperate again. 'I'm telling you I love you. Why won't you believe me? Is this something to do with that bastard Medford? You think I'm like him?'

'No,' she said. 'But…' She stared at him, her heart breaking. But she couldn't back down again, couldn't just accept this at face value. 'Maybe it is. I always thought I'd got over his rejection. That it didn't matter to me. But maybe I never stopped being that girl in some ways. Because I want to believe you, but I can't.'

He took her hand again and held it, his gaze steady, direct, unbreakable. 'Tell me what I need to do to make it right.'

She eased herself onto her elbows until she was sitting up. 'Can you…can you tell me what Daniel Smyth did to make you hate him so?'

'I don't hate him. I don't even care about him any more. I told you that,' he said, but she could hear the defensiveness. And knew she needed to know all of it if she was ever going to put her doubts to rest. She needed to know he trusted her enough to let her in. All the way in. It was a big ask. She got that. And maybe this was about her insecurities as much as his. But she deserved to know or she would never be able to let go of the thought that she was still just a port in a storm, someone he might decide to discard again.

'I know.' She touched his scarred cheek, her heart breaking as she felt him lean into the caress instinctively. 'And I believe you. But I still want to meet that boy. To know him. To understand him.'

So I can love all of him, if he'll let me.

'You don't want to know him. Believe me,' he said, the bitterness thick in his tone. 'He was a little—'

'No, he wasn't,' she interrupted him. 'He was scared and alone, the way I was. What did he do to you, Jack?'

'Daniel Smyth tried to force my mother to have an abortion.' The words guttered out, making the anguish tighten in her belly. *Oh, no.*

'She didn't, obviously, or I wouldn't be here. But that's how she ended up with my stepfather. She wasn't self-sufficient like you are,' he said, his voice so quiet, it barely registered. But still she felt the jolt of pride at the approval in his tone, her doubts starting to drift away. He had always seen her for who she really was, had always admired the things about her her father had despised. How could she have forgotten that?

'Is that why you insisted on marrying me?'

she asked, touched beyond belief. He had been showing her all along, who that boy was, and she hadn't even realised. 'Because he'd refused to help her?'

He stared at her, his gaze guarded again. 'Well, it's not the only reason.' He ran his palm over her belly again, caressing, sending the urgent desire through her body and making her smile. 'I wanted you. And… I needed you. But I didn't want to admit it. Not even to myself. Because it scared the hell out of me.'

'Oh, Jack.' She threw her arms around his neck, the happy tears flooding out—with no help whatsoever from the pregnancy hormones, for once. 'Yes. I love you. Let's be a family.'

'Wait a minute!' He drew back and held her at arm's length, his gaze confused. 'That's it? That's all you needed to hear?'

She nodded and grinned, despite the tears clogging her throat and rolling down her cheeks. 'I've been an idiot too. You showed me that boy. I just didn't see him. We're equals. That's all I needed know.'

'Thank God,' he said, then pulled her into his embrace and buried his face in her neck as she told him how much she loved him amidst watery kisses.

And when they finally got to look at their baby together for the first time, ten minutes later—and Jack bombarded poor Dr Patel with

a ton of questions it would never even have occurred to Katie to ask—Katie knew for sure
that neither of them would ever be alone again.

Because they had each other. Always.

EPILOGUE

Five months later

'WHAT BIG LUNGS you have, Master Wolfe.' Jack grinned down at the angry little face of the baby held securely in his arms as the tiny infant screwed up his eyes and launched into another angry, ear-splitting wail.

'All the better to drive us both mad with!' His wife grinned tiredly from the bed across the room.

'Shh, shh, little fella. It's okay. Daddy's here,' Jack said as he rocked the baby while crossing the room—to absolutely no avail. Young Master Wolfe was not happy. 'Sorry, Red,' he added, aware of how tired Katherine looked. 'I was hoping we wouldn't wake you.'

It was midnight. They'd only brought their son home this morning after Katherine had endured a twenty-two-hour labour. Jack adored his son to pieces, his awe and gratitude knowing no bounds when the baby had been handed o him after he'd cut the umbilical cord at the midwife's suggestion.

But no way in hell were they ever having another child. The labour had nearly killed him, and watching Katherine battle bravely through so much pain still had anxiety gripping his throat. He intended to wear condoms now for the rest of eternity.

If she ever wanted to sleep with him again, which was debatable. Because he wouldn't blame her in the slightest if she refused to allow him within ten feet of her naked body after what she'd been through less that twenty-four hours ago.

'It's okay,' Katherine murmured sleepily and sat up in bed—looking ludicrously serene and happy for a woman who had just survived what he considered to have been a major war.

Lifting her breast out of the feeding bra, exposing the plump nipple, she reached tired arms towards Jack. 'Give him to me,' she said, stifling a yawn. 'He probably just wants to feed.'

'Damn, seriously! He's done nothing but eat since we got home,' he murmured as he resolutely ignored the shot of arousal at the sight of his wife's glorious breast and handed her their precious little bundle of absolute fury.

The baby found the nipple, latched on immediately and began sucking furiously as if he'd been starved for hours, while his little fist finally stopped moving and settled against his wife's cleavage.

Another shot of arousal rippled through Jack's system...

What was wrong with him? Was he some kind of animal that he could get turned on by the perfectly natural sight of Katherine feeding their son?

'He's definitely a boob man, that's for sure,' Katherine said, her lips quirking in a cheeky smile that had his heart thumping his chest in hard, heady thuds. 'Not unlike his father.'

He chuckled, releasing the tension in his chest and letting go of the guilt.

God, but he loved this woman so much. How could she be so relaxed, so competent, taking this scary new experience called parenthood in her stride, when he was so useless? But he knew why. Because she was brave and smart and beautiful inside and out. And she had a wicked sense of humour that matched his own.

'Yeah, well, I hope he realises I'm gonna want those boobs back eventually,' Jack said wryly, joy bursting in his heart when she chuckled back.

'That may take a while, given how sore his mum is all over.'

'No worries,' Jack said, knowing if sexy banter was all he was going to get for a while it was more than enough. 'I can wait.'

She sent him a tender, welcoming smile as he climbed onto the bed beside her. He slung an arm around her shoulders and pulled her against his side, impossibly grateful for the companionship, the feeling of home she had created for him over the last five months...

He watched his son's cheeks gradually stop moving and the plump red nipple drop out of his mouth as he drifted back to sleep, as if by magic. Jack pressed a gentle kiss to his wife's temple while the wonder, the love—that was never far away when he watched his wife and child, his family—swelled in his chest, making it a little hard for him to breathe.

'Thank you, Mrs Wolfe,' he said softly.

'You're welcome, Mr Wolfe,' she whispered back. She lifted her head to smile at him. 'We really ought to give Master Wolfe a name, don't you think?' she said.

'How about Greedy?' he said.

She gave him a nudge in the ribs. 'I'm serious.'

'Okay, what do you want to call him?' Jack said, aware of a tickle of apprehension in his throat at the thought of this conversation. After all, the last time they'd discussed naming their son, he'd nearly torpedoed their whole relationship. 'I'm happy with anything you like,' he said, determined to make amends.

She gave him a patient, probing look. 'Okay. I like Aloysius.'

What the actual...?

'Okay,' he said, appalled and trying not to look it. 'Really?' he asked, when he spotted the mischievous twinkle in her eyes.

'No, not really... For goodness' sake, Jack. This is supposed to be a joint enterprise. I don't want to decide something so important on my own.'

'Okay,' he said carefully. But the apprehension still gripped his ribs. 'I just don't want to mess it up, like I did the last time.'

Katie stared at her husband and wanted to laugh and cry at the same time.

He'd been a wonderful father already. And an incredible partner over the last few months as they had navigated this stunning, life-altering and extremely scary experience together— of learning how to love each other, and how to prepare to become parents.

Not that there was really much you could do to prepare for something so momentous. She knew he was terrified of making a mistake, just like she was. She had seen how freaked out he'd been during the labour.

How much he already loved their son, though, and what an incredible father he was going to be, was plain to see. The mix of astonishmen

and tenderness on his face every time he held
the baby with such care, talked to him in that
deep, comforting and impossibly patient voice or
even changed a nappy with a ridiculous amount
of proficiency for a novice was both heart-melt-
ingly sweet and stupidly sexy.

But he still had insecurities. She knew that.
They both did. Insecurities which might take a
lifetime to overcome. After all, neither of them
had much of a blueprint for what a happy, con-
tented, functional family life even looked like,
let alone how to create it. She felt sure, though,
that they would figure it out... But only if they
figured it out together.

She sighed. 'You're not going to muck it up,
Jack. Unless you let me call the baby Aloysius
without an argument.'

He laughed and squeezed her shoulders.
'Point taken.'

His gaze drifted from her face and back to
their son, who was now sound asleep in her
arms. He touched a finger to the baby's downy
cheek, cleared his throat and murmured. 'You
said you liked Luca... Did you mean it?'

Her heart bounced against her ribs. 'You remembered that?' Why was she surprised, when
he had always been stupidly observant, even
when she didn't want him to be?

'Of course,' he said.

'Yes, I meant it. I love the name Luca,' she said.

He nodded. 'Good, because so do I.'

Kissing her tenderly on the lips—as her heart felt as if it were about to burst out of her chest with love—he held her securely in his embrace then murmured to their son. 'Hello, Luca Wolfe. Welcome to the family.'

* * * * *

Caught up in the magic of
A Baby to Tame the Wolfe?
Then don't miss these other Heidi Rice stories!

Innocent's Desert Wedding Contract
One Wild Night with Her Enemy
The Billionaire's Proposition in Paris
The CEO's Impossible Heir
Banished Prince to Desert Boss

Available now!